OPEN HOUSE

OPEN HOUSE

A NOVEL

Elizabeth Berg

BALLANTINE BOOKS • NEW YORK

A Ballantine Book
Published by The Ballantine Publishing Group
Copyright © 2000 by Elizabeth Berg

All rights reserved under International and Pan-American Copyright Conventions. Published in the United States by The Ballantine Publishing Group, a division of Random House, Inc., New York, and simultaneously in Canada by Random House of Canada Limited, Toronto.

Ballantine and colophon are registered trademarks of Random House, Inc.

www.randomhouse.com/BB/

A Library of Congress Catalog Card Number can be obtained from the publisher upon request.

ISBN 0-345-44550-3

This edition published by arrangement with Random House, Inc.

Manufactured in the United States of America

First Mass Market International Edition: March 2001

10 9 8 7 6 5 4 3 2

For Jean-Isabel McNutt

OPEN HOUSE

Prologue

YOU KNOW BEFORE YOU KNOW, OF COURSE. YOU ARE bending over the dryer, pulling out the still-warm sheets, and the knowledge walks up your backbone. You stare at the man you love and you are staring at nothing: he is gone before he is gone.

The last time I tried to talk to David was a couple of weeks ago. We were in the family room—David in his leather recliner, me stretched out on the sofa. Travis was asleep—he'd had his eleventh birthday party that afternoon, the usual free-for-all, and had fallen into bed exhausted. The television was on, but neither of us was watching it—David was reading the newspaper and I was rehearsing.

Finally, "David?" I said.

He looked up.

I said, "You know, you're right in saying we have some serious problems. But there are so many reasons to try to work things out." I hoped my voice was pleasant and light. I hoped my hair wasn't sticking up or that my nose didn't look too big and that I didn't look fat when I sat up a bit to adjust the pillow.

"I was wondering," I said, "if you would be willing to go to see someone with me, just once. A marriage counselor. I really think—"

"Samantha," he said.

And I said, "Okay."

He returned to the paper, and I returned to lying on the sofa, to falling down an elevator shaft. There were certain things I could not think about but kept thinking about anyway: how to tell the people I'd have to tell. How lonely the nights would be (that was a very long elevator shaft). How I believed so hard and for so long that we would be able to overcome everything, and now I would have to admit that we could not. How wrenching it is when the question you want to ask is "Why don't you *want* me?" but you cannot ask it and yet you do not ask—or talk about—anything else.

"David?" I said again, but this time he did not look up.

One

I DRESS TO BRING IN THE MORNING PAPER. THE NEW ME. I once read that Martha Stewart never wears a bathrobe. Not that I like Martha Stewart, nobody likes Martha Stewart, I don't think even Martha Stewart likes Martha Stewart. Which actually makes me like her. But anyway, maybe she's onto something. You get up, you make your bed right away, you shower and dress. Ready. Armed. Fire.

I go into the kitchen to make a strong pot of coffee and to start Travis's breakfast. French toast he'll have today, made from scratch, cut diagonally, one piece lying artfully over the other; and I'll heat the syrup, serve it in the tiny flowered pitcher I once took from a room-service tray. I'll cut the butter pats into the shape of something. A whale, maybe, he likes whales. Or a Corvette. If that doesn't work, I'll make butter curls with a potato peeler.

I lay out a blue linen place mat at the head of the dining-room table, smooth it with the flat of my hands, add a matching cloth napkin pulled through a wooden ring. *Wedding gift.* I center a plate, lay out the silverware, then step back to regard my arrangement. I really think Travis will appreciate this.

My head hurts. My head hurts, my heart hurts, my heart hurts. I stand still for a moment, which is dangerous.

So I go back into the kitchen, pull a dusty wineglass *wedding gift* down from the high cupboard above the refrigerator, wash it, and bring it to the dining room to center directly over the knife. Then I go back in the kitchen and select three oranges from the fruit bowl. I will squeeze them for juice just before he takes his seat.

Actually, Travis doesn't like fresh orange juice, but he's got to get used to elegance, because that's the way it's going to be from now on. Starting today. Well, starting last night, really, but Travis was asleep when the revolution started. I went to Bloomingdale's and charged a few things last night; that was the start; but when I got home, Travis had gone to bed.

I stand straighter, take in a deep breath. This is the first day. Every day that comes after this will be easier. Later, when I think of Travis sleeping, the thought will not pick up my stomach in its hands and twist it.

All right. Butter. The whale shape does not work, nor does the Corvette, but the butter curls do, more or less. I lay them carefully over ice chips in a small bowl, then bring them out to the dining room and place them to the right of his spoon. Is that where they go? There must be some incredibly expensive Martha Stewart book on table settings I can buy. Perhaps I'll hire a limo to take me to the bookstore, later—I don't really feel like driving. Perhaps I will take the limo to Martha's house. "I understand you're divorced," I'll say. "You seem to be doing all right."

Back in the kitchen, I gulp down another cup of coffee. Then I mix eggs and milk in a blue-and-yellow bowl *that tiny shop in Paris, our weeklong vacation there, I stood at the window one morning after I'd gotten up and he came up behind me and put his arms around my middle, his lips to the back of my neck,* add a touch of vanilla, a sprinkle of sugar. I put a frying pan on the stove *put his lips to the back of my neck and we went back to bed*, lay out two slices of bread on the cutting board. These hands at the ends of my wrists remove the crusts. I'm not sure why. Oh, I know why. Because they're hard.

I sit down at the table. Stand up. Sit down. Concentrate on my breathing, that's supposed to help.

Actually, it does not.

I check my watch. Good, only five more minutes. I take off my apron and go upstairs to my bathroom. I brush my teeth again, put in my contacts, comb my hair, apply eyeliner, mascara, and a tasteful shade of red lipstick. I straighten the cowl neck of my new sweater. It's red, too—cashmere. I dab a little Joy—also new—behind my ears and on my wrists. Then I stand still, regard myself as objectively as possible in the mirror.

Well, I look just fine. Okay, circles under the eyes, big deal. The main thing is, what a wonderful change for Travis! Instead of him seeing me in my usual old bathrobe with the permanent egg stain on the left lapel, I am nicely dressed, made up, and ready to go. *Everything* will be different, starting today. Everything will be better.

I go into Travis's room. He is messily asleep; covers wrapped around one leg, pajama top hiked high on his back, pillows at odd angles, his arm hanging over one side of the bed.

"Travis?" I say softly, raising his shade. "It's seven o'clock." I sit down beside him, rub his back. "Travis?"

"I'm up," he says sleepily. Then, turning over quickly, eyes wide, "What *stinks*?" He puts his hand over his nose.

I stand; step back. "Perfume, it's . . . Listen, get dressed and come down for breakfast, okay? I'm making French toast."

No reaction.

"I mean, not the frozen kind. From scratch." *Please, Travis.*

He sits up, rubs his head. Two blond cowlicks stick up like devil horns. He is wearing one of David's T-shirts with his own pajama bottoms. The bottoms are too short for him, I see now. Well. No problem. Today I will replace them. Maybe Ralph Lauren makes pajama bottoms for kids. Silk ones. Monogrammed.

Travis yawns again, hugely, scratches his stomach. I look away, despairing of this too manly movement. It seems so recent that I had to step around imaginative arrangements of Legos—jagged-backed dinosaurs, secret space stations, tools for "surgery"—to wake him up. Now he hides a well-thumbed issue of *Playboy* under his bed. One day when Travis was at school, I inspected Miss August thoroughly. I felt like putting in a note for the next time he looked at her:

Dear Travis, Please be advised that this is not a real woman. These are bought boobs, and pubic hair looks nothing like this in its natural state. This woman needs to find her life's work and not spend all of her time in front of a mirror. If you went out with her, you would soon be disappointed. Signed, a caring friend.

"I don't want French toast," Travis says. "I want Cheerios."

"You have Cheerios every day."

"Right. Be*cause,* you see, I *like* them."

Sarcastic. Like David. But he is smiling, saying this. It is David's smile, born again.

"Well, today is a special day," I tell him.

"How come?"

"We'll talk about that later."

"Okay, but I don't want French toast."

"Why don't you just try—"

"*Pleeeeeeeease????*"

My God. You'd think he was begging for a stay of execution.

"Fine." I make my mouth smile, make myself walk slowly down the stairs, one foot, then the other. I am wearing panty hose under my new jeans, and I feel the fabrics rubbing together as if each is questioning the other's right to be there.

I go into the family room *pipe tobacco* and turn the stereo on to the classical station. Ah, Mozart. Well, maybe not Mozart. But close enough. It's one of those guys. I'll take a music appreciation class. Somewhere. Then, getting ready to sit down to dinner with Travis some night I'll say, "Some Verdi, perhaps?"

"That's an idea," he'll answer. "But maybe Vivaldi would be better with lamb."

"You know, you're absolutely right," I'll say. I will have taught him this exquisite discrimination. As a famous man, Travis will say to the interviewer, "My mother changed wonderfully when my father left us. Our circumstances actually improved. Naturally I owe her everything."

In the dining room, I remove Travis's plate from the table, then go into the kitchen to pour Cheerios into a bowl. Too plain. I'll slice some banana on top in a most beautiful way. I pick up a knife, and some feeling comes over me that has me rush over to the kitchen table. I sit and hold the knife and try very hard to stifle a sob. *Not now. Later.* And then something occurs to me: David may change his mind. That's why he didn't insist on telling Travis himself, right away. He's not sure he even wants to do this. This is male menopause, early male menopause, it could be that, they get that just like they get their own version of PMS, they just don't admit it. He's been so moody, I haven't been good about listening to him, I haven't been willing to talk about a lot of things I do wrong. He could very well have needed to just act out this way, scare himself a little—well, scare both of us—and now he'll come back and we'll just straighten this out. Men! I get up, Lucy Ricardo.

I take a banana from the fruit bowl, slice it evenly, ignore the feeling of a finger tapping my shoulder. *Sam? He's not coming back.*

I look at my watch, pour milk into the pitcher I was going to use for the syrup. Then I pick a pink blossom off the begonia plant on the kitchen windowsill to rest beside his plate. I carry everything out to the dining room, carefully arrange it, then lean against the doorjamb. Outside, the sun shines. Birds call. Cars pass with the windows down, people's elbows hanging out.

I am exhausted.

It will be a few minutes before Travis comes down. I need to do something.

I go into the basement to start a load of wash. When I begin separating, I find a pair of David's boxer shorts, the blue ones, and, God help me, I bury my face in them for the smell of him.

I look up and see my sewing machine. I bring his shorts over to it. Then, using a hidden seam, I sew the fly shut. With great care, I do this, with tenderness. Then I go back to the pile of laundry and get some of his fancy socks and sew the tops of them shut.

I have a lot of David's clothes to choose from; he packed last evening like he was only going on a business trip for a couple of days. And I sat on the bed watching him, thinking *Why is he packing? Where is he going?*

Why must he do it like this, does he think he's in a movie? What can I say to stop this, isn't there something to say to stop this? But I couldn't say anything. I felt paralyzed. And when he finally stood at the doorway of the bedroom and said, "I'll call you," I'd waved. Waved! Then, from the bedroom window, I'd watched him drive away, marveling at his cool efficiency in signaling at the corner.

I could not stay in the house alone. I would not stay in the house. Travis was gone—he went to his friend Ben's house every Thursday after school to eat dinner and do homework. He liked going there because that family had three dogs and a cat, whereas, as Travis frequently liked to point out, he had nothing, not even ants. I called my mother, telling her briefly what had happened and asking her to come over and wait for Travis to get home. And then I got in the car and drove to the mall and charged and charged and charged.

When I got home my mother assured me that, as requested, she had not said anything to Travis. Amazingly, she said little to me, either. "We'll talk later, honey," she said, and I answered in what I hoped was a noncommittal way. I was so grateful she had come. I wanted so much for her to go.

I come up from the laundry room and find Travis seated at the dining-room table, delicately picking the banana off his Cheerios. "How come I'm eating out here?" he asks.

"For fun."

"Can I have some orange juice?"

"Oh! Yes, I forgot, I'll go make it right now."

". . . You're making it?"

"Yes. You're having fresh-squeezed orange juice."

"I don't like fresh-squeezed orange juice. I mean, I'm

sorry, but you *know* I don't like it. It's got all that stuff floating around that bumps into your teeth. Plus I don't like *bananas* on my cereal, *either*."

"Travis. Listen to me. You must try new things every now and then. Sometimes you have learned to like things in your sleep."

"Are we out of Tropicana?"

"Yes, we are."

He gets up and goes to the refrigerator, peers in, tri-umphantly pulls out a carton of juice. "It's right here, Mom, practically full! We're not out of it! See?"

I take the carton from him, upend it over the sink. "Now we are."

We stand there. Finally, "*Jesus!*" he says. "What's wrong with *you*?"

Let's see. Let's see. What to do.

"Come with me," I say. I lead him to the dining room, point to his chair. "Finish your cereal, okay? It's almost time to go."

I sit down with him, take in a breath. "I'm sorry about the orange juice, Travis. I'm really sorry I did that. That wasn't right."

I clasp my hands together, stare at him. He has a bit of sleep stuck in one corner. "Wipe your left eye," I tell him. "You need to wash your face a little better in the morning. And, listen, I don't want you saying 'Jesus' like that."

"*You* do." He wipes at his right eye.

"Other eye."

"*Dad* does. *He* does it all the time."

I sit still. Outside, I see the wind lift up a branch, rock it. Then let it go.

Finally, I say, "I don't care who does it, Travis. It's not okay for you to do it. Don't say it anymore."

"Fine."

I lean back in my chair, sigh.

"What's *wrong*?" he asks.

"There is something wrong."

"I *said*."

"Right. But I don't want you to worry. I'm going to talk to you about it, okay? But I think it would be best if we waited until after school."

"Are you . . . going somewhere, Mom?"

I don't answer right away. I don't know. Am I?

Worried now, "How come you're all dressed already? Are you going to the doctor or something?" Someone in Travis's grade had lost his mother recently. The knowledge festered among the kids, spooked them terribly despite the carefully planned programs presented by the guidance counselors.

There, I am suddenly grounded. It is such sweet, wavelike relief. "Oh, sweetie, no, it's nothing like that. It's nothing like that! I'm sorry, I know I'm acting . . . I'm just tired. But we'll talk later. It'll be fine." I smile brightly. "So! Did you like eating breakfast this way?"

"What way?"

"Well . . . You know, out here in the dining room. Fancy dishes . . ."

"Yeah, I guess so. Yeah! It was nice. Thanks, Mom."

Oh, what am I doing? Why am I making him take care of *me*?

Travis picks up his book bag, then shifts his shoulders, seeming to adjust himself inside himself, a gesture I love.

"Can I kiss you good-bye?" I ask.

Our old joke. Every morning I ask him this, and every morning (since he turned nine, anyway) he makes a face as though I were asking him if I could spoon cold oatmeal into his ear. But now he nods yes and my stomach does an unpleasant little somersault. I put my lips to his cheek. And he kisses me back—pecks at my cheek and then quickly turns away.

So. He knows. They are absolutely right, kids always know. When he comes home from school today and I tell him that David has moved out, he will nod sadly and say, "I thought so." And then he will start making *F*s.

I watch him walk down the sidewalk toward school. His jacket collar is half up, half down. His jeans are slightly too long; they bunch up over the top of his sneakers. His book bag carries papers with his earnest script, his own thoughts about the material he is assigned to read. He is just beginning to become himself. He is too young to have to face what he is going to have to face, it will shape him too much, quash his tender optimism. It's unfair, it's so un*fair*! That's what I should have told David: do what you have to do, but don't walk out on Travis. For God's sake. Ruin my world if you have to, but don't ruin his, too.

Back in the kitchen, I take a sip from my coffee. It's gone cold; a ring of congealed cream visible at the outside edge. Look how fast things turn. I dump the coffee out, then throw the cup in the trash. I never want to see that cup again. "David," I say, very softly. Like a prayer. "David," I say again, and lean against the wall to cry. It helps. It's so funny, how it helps. Stress hormones get released when you cry, that's why it works. It's amazing how smart the body is. Though maybe we could do without loving. I think it's overrated, and I think it's too hard. You should only love your children; that is necessary, because otherwise you might kill them. But to love a man? It's overrated, and it's too hard and I will never, ever do it again.

Well. What I will do now is make a list. There's a lot to

think about, so much to do. I'll go outside, I'll sit out there where it's so much bigger, where there is no roof to fall in on your head and make you brain damaged, should you survive.

AT THREE-THIRTY, I am sitting on the sofa in the family room, waiting for Travis. I've had a nap, I'm fine. Well, I've had a couple of naps. The waking-up part, that's hard. *What's . . . ?* Oh. *Oh, yes.*

One thing I want to be sure of is that Travis does not blame himself in any way. I believe I should start with that. Out loud, I practice, "Travis, sweetie, I need to tell you some things that will be hard for you to hear." Yes. Good. "But what I want you to understand, and to re-member the whole time I'm talking, is this: all of this is about your *father and me*. This decision. It has nothing to do with you. You are such a good boy." Yes.

No. No. This is starting with a negative. It will scare him. Start with something positive. "Travis, as I'm sure you know, both your father and I love you very much." No. That will scare him, too. Oh, what then? *Guess what, Travis? Your father left us and now we get to have a whole new life! Do you want a dog? I was never the one who objected to pets, you know. Do you want a Newfoundland? I think they weigh about five hundred pounds, do you want one of them?*

The door opens and Travis comes in, sees me from the hallway. "Hi, Mom." *The last normal thing.*

"Oh. Hi! Hi, honey."

He regards me warily. "Are you . . . ?"

"I'm fine!"

He nods, heads toward the kitchen.

"What are you doing?"

"Getting a snack. Do you want some pretzels?"

"No, thanks." I cross my legs, fold my hands on my lap. Uncross my legs.

"Travis?"

"Yeah?"

"Why don't you put your pretzels in a bowl, okay?"

Silence.

"Travis?"

He comes into the room, holding the bag of pretzels. "What do I need a bowl for? The bag is fine, I always eat out of the bag."

"Well, it's . . ." *Inelegant*, is what I want to say. I would like to say that, I have always liked that word. And I have to tell him that we need to make some changes here; things are going to change. But, "The bag is fine," I say. And then, "Could you come here, please?"

He walks over slowly, sits beside me, offers me the bag of pretzels.

"No, thanks."

"They're a little stale."

"Travis," I begin.

"I know. You're getting a divorce." He looks up at me, sighs.

I sit back, smile.

"Aren't you?"

"Well, yes, we just—"

"I figured."

". . . You figured."

"Yeah."

"Why?"

He puts his finger in his ear, experimentally, it seems. Twists it.

"Travis?"

"Huh?"

"*Why* did you 'figure'?"

"I don't know. Everybody gets divorced."

"Oh no. Not everyone. There are many, many happy marriages. I'm sure you'll have one. But your father and I have decided that . . . yes, we want a divorce, and so we're going to be living apart from one another. Starting . . . Well, actually starting last night."

"Where is he?"

"He's close by, he's at a hotel in town, he called me this afternoon. And he'll be calling you tonight, Travis, he told me to tell you he'd be calling you after dinner. And that he will be seeing you very soon."

"What time?"

"Pardon?"

"What time will he call?"

"I don't think he said that. I think he just said after dinner."

"Yeah, but what does that *mean*, what *time* does that mean?"

"Um . . . Okay. It must . . . I think about seven, right around seven. All right?"

"Why is he at a *hotel*?"

Beats me. "He . . . Well, you know, honey, when people decide they aren't going to be together any longer, they often need a little time apart, to think about things."

"But you're getting divorced!"

"Yes."

"So you'll *be* apart!"

"Yes, but—there just sometimes has to be this—"

"Whatever. I don't care."

"Oh, Travis, I'm so sorry."

He shrugs, inspects his thumb, the wall. "It's all right." His right knee starts bouncing up and down and I have to stop myself from stopping it.

When Travis was six, he fell off a jungle gym and hurt

his arm. The X-ray technician kept telling him to hold his arm a certain way—it required a kind of twisting. Travis kept saying he couldn't do it, and the impatient tech finally went into the room with him and *made* his arm go the way she wanted it to. "Now, *keep* it like that until I get the picture," I heard her say. When Travis came out of the room, he had tears in his eyes, and when he saw me, he began crying. A little later, when the X-rays were hung, the doctor saw that there was a break right where the tech had been twisting. "That must have *hurt*," the doctor said, "holding your arm that way." Travis nodded gravely. He wasn't crying anymore. He'd been given a lollipop and a sticker that said *I just got an X-ray!*

"Travis, it's not all right. I want you to know that Dad and I both know that. And we also want you to understand that this decision had nothing to do with you." *I just got taken off the hook for my parents' divorce!*

"I know that."

"Do you?"

"Yeah. Why would it have to do with me?"

"Well, that's absolutely right, Travis. We both love you very much, and we will both continue to be your parents. It's just that Dad and I can't live together anymore."

"*Why?*"

"Well . . ." *Sometimes people, even when they really love each other, they kind of grow apart. And it becomes very hard to . . .* "Because your father is a very, very selfish person who thinks only of himself. Always has, always will. He deserted me, Travis, just like that. I had no idea he was so unhappy. I don't know what I'm going to do. I don't know what to do. I really hate him for this. I *hate* him!" I put my hand to my mouth, start to cry. "Oh, Travis, I'm sorry."

"I'm going upstairs to my room for a while."

"Wait. I—"

"Mom, please?"

"Yes, all right." A weight attaches itself to my chest, sinks in. And in. Maybe it's a heart attack. I hope it is.

Travis walks quickly up the stairs. I hear his door close. I hold one of my hands with the other, stare out the window. Sit there. Sit. When I see the sun beginning to go down, I head up to his bedroom. On the pretense of asking what he'd like for dinner.

Tomorrow morning I will call someone for help.

To think that I asked David to let me be the one to tell Travis, and to let me be alone, telling him. I should have known better. I don't blame David for leaving me, I would like to leave me, too. I would like to step into the body of a woman who does not get lost going around the block, who does not smell of garlic for three days after she eats it, who can make conversation with David's clients at a restaurant rather than going into the ladies' room to sit in the stall and find things in her purse to play with. David has never liked my mother, who is just plain foolish, or my best friend, Rita, who does not censor her thoughts enough to suit him. Gray hair is popping out all over my head, I have become intimately acquainted with cellulite, and just last week, I awakened to hear myself snoring. I want to leave, too. But I can't.

I go upstairs and knock on Travis's door. There is a moment. Then he calls, "Come in," and I can feel the relief clear to the edges of my scalp.

Two

❖

WHENEVER THE PHONE RINGS, I ANSWER IT AS IF THE rescuers have appeared in a helicopter above me and are lowering the rope. "Hello?" I say, meaning, *Please.* It is never the rescuers. It is a cheerful young girl wanting to know if I would like to contribute to the ballet. Not this year, I say. It is Monica Kaplan, asking if I'd like to contribute a dozen cupcakes for the bake sale coming up in October. I'll bring a few dozen, I say. And now it is my mother.

"Honey, you have got to get right back on the horse. I mean it. I don't say you're not hurting, God knows I know that, but you've got to get right out there and start dating. You're still a young woman, forty-two is nothing—you're an infant."

It is twelve noon. I am sitting at the kitchen table with a stack of mail-order catalogues and an empty box of Godiva chocolates, which I now know are seriously overrated. Also with an empty Scotch glass, but I didn't put much in there. Hardly anything. I pull the telephone away from my ear and lay it on my chest, breathe out a long sigh. I wish I hadn't told my mother so soon. But I had to.

I put the phone back to my ear. "Ma, I'm not ready to *date*. For God's sake. I couldn't care less about that. I just want to figure out how to keep Travis . . . safe." I look at the Scotch glass, turn it upside down.

"Well, he's *safe*, Sam, he's with his *mother*. Of course he's safe! And despite what you may think, children are really very, very resilient. You'd be surprised. I can tell you with all certainty that what Travis wants right now is for you to go on with your life. That's what will help him the most. He doesn't want to see you mooning around, doing nothing. You haven't cried in front of him, have you? For God's sake, don't *cry* in front of him, whatever you do. He's taking his cues from you: if you're happy, he'll be happy. Think of it as your job to pick yourself up and get going again. Why, when your father died, I didn't waste any time. I went right out and started meeting people."

"Meeting men, you mean."

"Well, *yes*. Of course. It's the natural thing. Woman needs man and man needs woman, and that's all there is to it, I don't care what anybody says. For the homosexuals, of course, it's a little different, but it's still the same, anyway."

". . . What?"

"Oh, you know what I mean. The point is, if a child sees his mother dating, it lets him know that she's special. And then of course *he* feels special, too. I'm not making this up. Just think back to how you girls felt when I dated. You didn't mind at all. You liked it."

I close my eyes, rub my forehead. Where to start? I remember distinctly sitting at the kitchen table eating dinner with my sister, Louise, a few months after our father died. We were having macaroni and cheese with hot dogs sliced into it. While we ate, our mother sat at the table with us, doing her nails. She had a date that evening, and her hair was in pin curls, covered with a bright yellow kerchief. She chewed ice cubes from a sweating aluminum tumbler while she painted each fingernail a thrilling red.

She was going out to dinner. To a *very* nice restaurant, she said, that she'd heard all about. There was a live orchestra at that restaurant, men in tuxedos, and oh, the violins were supposed to be fantastic! There was a little lamp on the table that you turned on whenever you wanted the waiter to come. When they brought the check, they presented it along with a red rose for the lady—long-stemmed!

Our mother tried to date at least three times a week. She marked her calendar with red Xs and names, keeping a desperate tally. Tonight was Wolfgang Mueller ("Wolfie," she called him), a wholesale meat man who had the unfortunate habit of spitting a bit when he talked. He was a very tall man, with black eyebrows that seemed intent on escaping his face—they grew straight out a good half-inch. "You could land an *airplane* there!" Louise said, the first time we met him. The hot dogs we were eating were a gift from him, presented to our mother the last time they went out. "For you, my Veronica," he'd said, bowing slightly and handing her the meat, wrapped in white butcher's paper and tied with red-and-white striped string. "Und here, you zee," he said, pointing proudly, "I hef made the schtring so as to look like a little mouze. Here we hef little ears, here is das body, und here, the tail! You zee?"

"Oh, *Wolfie!*" my mother had said. And then she had shown Louise and me the package, saying, "Look. Can you see the mouse Wolfie made for you?" I stared in vain, and Louise left the room. "Next he'll show up here in *lederhosen*," she told me later.

I was ten then, young enough to believe that hot dogs

mixed with macaroni was fine dining, and to be thoroughly captivated by the idea of dating—if not by the men you had to spend time with in order to do it. As I saw it, the men were pretty much beside the point; it was the getting ready part that mattered.

On a day when she had a date, my mother pored through magazines to find the style most appropriate for that evening, then washed and set her hair. About an hour before pick-up time, she took a lengthy bubble bath. She emerged in a warm cloud of fragrance, then sat at her dressing table, rolled up her robe sleeves, and went to work. I would sit on her bed playing with Betsy McCall paper dolls and watching my mother style her hair in one updo or another, bobby pins clamped between her teeth. Next she applied foundation in smooth, upward strokes to her face and neck, even to the back of her neck. She put a dot of rouge on each cheek, then rubbed it in for a quick blossoming of color—that was my favorite part. She applied her mascara carefully, her mouth open; then darkened her eyebrows. Next lipstick, laid on thickly, blotted on a tissue. She screwed on sparkly earrings, turned her head left and right. She would anoint herself with My Sin, and then slip into a dress that came from a plastic protector.

"How do I look?" she would always ask, turning on her tiptoes like the ballerina on my jewelry box. And I would always answer—truthfully—*beautiful*. I was sad when she was ready to go—the delicious sounds of clicking bottles and rustling fabrics would be gone, her rich scent would fade, and I would be left with Louise, whose idea of being a good baby-sitter was to let me do things for her.

I did not yet agree with Louise that our mother was absolutely mortifying—at least not all of the time. I did not agree that we should run away to New Jersey to live with our father's relatives, all of whom were much more dignified than our mother. I was still tucked in at night, still wanted, at that time, to have my mother stay and stay beside me.

Louise, on the other hand, was fourteen, newly free of needing primal comfort and therefore deeply scornful of it; she spent most of her time locked in her room. Perhaps more than anything, Louise hated our mother's going out with men she called the goons. She was so *obvious* about it, Louise told me; she was so *eager* to take up with *anyone* who came along. And it pained me too, it did. Louise and I had adored our father, a good-looking and gentle man who died with open-eyed surprise from a heart attack at forty-one. But we said nothing to our mother.

But now, finally, I do. "No, in fact we *hated* your dating. It didn't make us feel better at all."

"Oh, of course it did," my mother says. I know the gesture that will accompany this remark: Veronica will reach up to the right side of her face and adjust a few pieces of the red hair curled there. Emphatically. I used to wonder why there weren't fingerprint-sized dents all along the side of her face.

I stretch the phone cord out to dump the candy box in the trash. "Listen, I appreciate your concern, I really do, but I don't want advice just yet, okay? For one thing, it's a different situation entirely. David isn't dead."

My mother sniffs. "As far as I'm concerned, he is."

"You know, Ma, I only called to see if you could stay with Travis for a while this afternoon, maybe make him dinner if I'm not back in time. Could you do that, do you think?"

"Of course I can. I have a pedicure at one-thirty; I'll be able to get there long before he's home from school."

"All right. So I'll see you when I get home. Sometime around . . . I don't know. Sometime."

"Sam?"

"Yes?"

"Where are you going, honey? You sound a little . . . You're not going to a therapist, are you? They're crazier than the rest of us, really they are. I knew a woman— well, actually, you might remember her, Louise Castlebaum? Always trying to show off her legs, which, in my opinion, were not so worthy of showing off, but *anyway*, *she* went to a therapist—a full-blown *psychiatrist*!— and—"

"Ma! I'm not going to a therapist! I'm going . . ." *Nuts.* "I'm going shopping."

"Well, now. That's better! That's a *very* good thing to do! Just forget about things, indulge yourself a little!" Then, her tone shifting, "And what should I say if David calls? Should I say you're out with someone else?"

They should keep a permanent chair empty for my mother in some sixth-grade classroom. Stencil her name on it. She'd be so comfortable there.

"David is not going to call," I tell her.

"What makes you so sure?"

"Because, if you must know, he told me very clearly that he wanted us to have a week of no communication before we talked any more. At all. About anything. He is talking to Travis, but not to me."

"Oh. I see."

"All right, Mother?"

"All right. Sam?"

"I really have to go."

"Real quick, now, just listen. You're going out anyway,

right? I have an extra coupon for a pedicure, you could swing by Stephano's and get one with me. Wouldn't cost you anything, not a cent, even the tip is included. I know you think it's silly, but really, a good pedicure can do you a world of good, change your whole outlook. When your feet feel good, you do, too. This could be just the ticket."

"I don't think so. But thanks."

I hang up the phone, go upstairs to dress. Once, after I broke up with my high school sweetheart, my mother bought me pedal pushers. She came into my bedroom where I'd been weeping, holding them up and swaying them from side to side. "Look what's back in style," she said. "With a cute little pair of *san*dals?" When I didn't respond, she sat on the bed beside me, put her arm around me. "Well, honey, what is it? Don't you like yellow? I thought they were so cheerful. But I swear, they *have* every color under the sun. I can go back right now and exchange them. How about purple? Would that do it?" She squeezed me, leaned over to look into my face, wiped some tears away. "Pink?"

When we were roommates in college, Rita had once asked, extremely gently, if my mother were mentally retarded. "No," I said. "Just . . . Southern." That was the only explanation I could come up with at the time. And I still make do with it.

Three

◆

THE SALESMAN AT TIFFANY'S IS WEARING A NAVY BLUE
suit, a beautiful red silk tie, and a white shirt with discreet blue stripes. Also monogrammed cuff links: gold,
with a rich patina. He is half bald, red-nosed; a drinker, I
suppose, though an elegant one, who makes his martinis
in a Baccarat pitcher before he passes out from them
every night. Perhaps I'll buy one of those pitchers, too.

Thus far I have ordered a Limoges china tea set. It is for
me to use in the late afternoons. I will sit by a window that
has good light and that will also, very soon, have French
lace curtains. Or Belgian, whatever's more expensive.

After some deliberation, I selected the American Garden
china pattern. I liked the drooping petals of the scattered
and varied flowers, the hopeful green curl of the leaves that
surrounded them. The thin, outer ring of gold ("Fourteen
karat?" I asked. "Twenty-three, madam," he answered)
around the edge of the plate was beautiful next to the inner
ring of a rich navy blue.

I never wanted such things before, and David was
indifferent—he'd had enough of it all growing up. But
now I do want them. I'm not sure why. Well, yes I do
know why. I want them because they cost a fortune, and
I think David should have to pay. Such a cliché—you
break my heart and I break the bank.

Now I'm looking at silver, I want a teaspoon to accompany the tea set. *Sugar?* I will ask myself. *Oh yes, please,* I will answer. The man has recommended a floral pattern for the silver, something also called American Garden, but I actually prefer Audubon, which features birds, as well as flowers. "Would that work?" I ask the man, and he stares slightly past me as he answers, "Of course, you *could* do that . . ."

Ah.

On the back of my heel is a messy Band-Aid from where I cut myself shaving this morning—I feel as though that Band-Aid has migrated onto my forehead. I would like to step into the body of a woman who knows how to order silver. Also I would like to step into the body of a woman whose insides do not feel as though they have been spending time against the fine side of a cheese grater.

After an awkward moment I say, "I think I'll just go ahead with the American Garden design. Now, a teaspoon is ninety dollars, is that right?"

"That's correct."

"Uh-huh." *Jesus!* "And . . . let me just ask you, a complete place setting of this silver would be . . ."

"Four hundred and eighty-five dollars, for the four pieces. Plus tax, of course."

"Four pieces?"

"Yes. That's the two forks, a knife, and a spoon."

"No dessert spoon?"

"That would be extra. A dessert spoon would be another one hundred and twenty-five dollars."

"Oh. Right. And so a five-piece setting would be . . ."

"Six hundred and ten dollars."

"I see." Ever so slightly, my stomach begins hurting. The man waits, standing so straight and still I wonder for a moment if he is mechanized, a little Tiffany's trick that nearly succeeds due to the verisimilitude of the reddened nose. But no, there, he is exhaling real air. I sense an extremely polite impatience. He knows I'm a fake; he doesn't think I can afford any of this. Well, he's absolutely right. I can't. But the bill will go to David.

"Suppose I wanted an entire silver setting," I say.

A light in the pale blue eyes. "For . . ."

I feel the color rise in my face. Has he understood? Does he know what I'm doing? Do I? "Well, I just . . . like it."

"Oh yes, understandably, of course. But . . . Place settings, I meant. Service for . . ."

"Oh! Yes. For . . . six?"

He nods, smiles. His teeth cross endearingly in the front. I can see the tracks of his comb through his hair. I wonder if Vitalis is back in style. Should I tell Travis to start using it? Oh, too much is *on* me now.

"I'll tell you what," I say. "Let's make it service for ten." There. Now I feel better.

"Could you excuse me for just one moment?" the man asks. "I'll get my calculator. And I need to go in back for some more order forms. It will be just a moment."

I give a grand wave of dismissal. Queen Elizabeth. Elizabeth Taylor. "Take your time," I tell him. "I'll just look around."

I put the sample teacup back carefully on the lighted display shelf, then move over to the jewelry. I walk past emerald rings, ruby rings, diamond necklaces, gold watches. Past whimsical pins: bejeweled sea horses and dragonflies, bees and frogs. I stop to admire long strands of lambent pearls draped over black velvet. Uniformed guards watch me from the corners of their eyes, their arms loosely crossed. I try on a channel-set sapphire-and-diamond necklace. Then I try on a bracelet, an

Étoile twist, eighteen-karat gold, studded with diamonds
set in platinum. I turn my wrist this way and that, watching the light bounce off the stones. Very nice. "And this is
how much?" I ask the young woman helping me.

"Three thousand, five hundred dollars." She is wearing
a gray suit with matching heels, pearl studs. And a ring
with an acorn-sized diamond; it must be borrowed from
the store. Her hairdo, a tightly wound twist, is much too
severe. To say nothing of her demeanor. This woman
needs to get out and play more. Although maybe she does
play. Maybe this job, in fact, is playing. Maybe she lives
in a dump with three wild roommates and tells them sto-
ries about the dipshits who shop at Tiffany. I hope so.

"That bracelet looks wonderful on you," the woman
says. "It suits you."

The standard line.

But "It does, doesn't it?" I say. "I'll take it. I'll wear it
out. We'll just add it to the other purchases."

"Certainly," the woman says, and nods to the man
across the aisle in china, who has resumed his post. He
stands politely waiting. When I go back over to him, he
looks at the bracelet. "Lovely selection. Very elegant."

"Thank you," I say. There's no reason in the world for
me not to wear things like this. I have always liked the
look of blue jeans and diamonds; I, too, can wear them.
This will be my everyday bracelet, my signature piece.

"Here's how it all breaks down." The man shows me
the figures for the cost of the silver and china. With the
cost of the bracelet, my total will be over twelve thousand dollars. *Twelve thousand!* The number zips a finger
up my spine, thrills me deeply in a way that reminds me
of sex. From what I can recall.

"Well, I . . . My goodness!" I say, and start laughing.
And then stop. My fingers wander to the area behind my

ear. An old, nervous habit: the body seeking a consultation with the body. *"Whew!"*

Silence from the man. From the whole store, it seems.

Finally, "I . . . Oh, God. I'm sorry," I say. I take the bracelet off, lay it on the counter. "I think maybe I should just go with the tea set, okay? And the one teaspoon, as I had originally planned. Would that be all right?"

"Of course."

I don't know how people fall out of love, Sam. It's an old story, isn't it? The fact is, I can't endure any of this any longer. "Endure." He actually said that.

"Or . . . You know what?" I tell the man. "Let me have it all." I put the bracelet back on, lean in closer to him. "Thought you'd lost me there, huh?"

"Oh, no. Not at all. It's a big decision."

"What's your name?"

"My name?" Three long fingers to his breastbone, shyly. Oh, he's sweet. Why didn't I marry someone like him? "It's James."

"I'm Samantha. Sam."

"I'm glad to meet you."

"I'll bet you are."

He looks up. "No, I mean . . . apart from that."

"Well. Thank you." I swallow away a sudden tightening in my throat, pull out my checkbook. I need new checks. I need, I need, I need, I need.

DRIVING HOME, I pass a young black woman standing at the side of the road with a little girl, perhaps four years old. The woman is holding up a sign that says, "Will work for food." I pull over to the curb, lower the window. The woman approaches me hesitantly.

"Here," I say, holding the bracelet out to her. "Don't

get ripped off, selling it. It's real. It's worth three thousand, five hundred dollars."

The woman looks at the bracelet, then at me.

"Take it," I say.

She shakes her head, mutters something, walks away.

"Hey!" I call after her.

She keeps walking.

I cut the engine, get out of the car, and run after her. "Wait! I want to *give* you this! It's real! I'm not kidding!"

The woman turns slowly. "You a cop or something?"

"No, I am not." My breathing is ragged. How did I get so out of shape?

"You crazy, then?"

"Mommy?" the child says softly.

"Just a minute, baby. Hold on." Then, to me, "What's your deal anyway? I take the bracelet, you shoot me in the back, is that it?"

"Mommy, I have to *pee*," the little girl says.

"I know, I'm going to take you, we going home in just a minute." The woman stares at me through narrowed eyes, considering. She has a lovely face, a missing tooth near the front of her mouth. She is wearing a burgundy sweatshirt, yellow corduroy pants, a dirty jean jacket with half its buttons missing. The little girl wears newer sneakers and blue jeans, a down jacket zipped to her chin, though the October evening is mild.

"I just bought this," I say. "But I . . . don't want it. I want to give it to you."

"*Shit*. For real?"

"Yes."

The woman shrugs, takes the bracelet, and quickly shoves it into her pocket.

The little girl, who had been hiding behind her mother's leg, peeks out. "My name is Tiffany."

"Is that right?" There you are, this was meant to be.

The woman reaches out to touch my arm. "God bless you," she says, her eyes full of tears.

I can think of nothing to say. I watch the woman and her daughter walk away, then call out, "Did you need a ride?"

The woman turns around, keeps walking backward. "No, ma'am. We almost there. But thank you. God bless you, now."

I get back into my car, pull out into the traffic.

I don't know, I feel good. I don't know why I bought that bracelet. In my jewelry box are a fair number of velvet cases holding necklaces and bracelets that David gave me for my birthday, for Christmas. But I don't like fancy jewelry; I never have. The fancy things I like are sheets. Pots and pans. And the things I *really* like aren't fancy at all: old aprons and hankies. Butter wrappers from the one-pound blocks. Peony bushes, hardback books of poetry. And I like things *less* than that; the sticky remains at the bottom of the apple-crisp dish. The way cats sometimes run sideways. The presence of rainbows in a puddle of oil. Mayonnaise jars. Pussy willows. Wash on a line. The *tick-tock* of clocks, the blue of the neon sign at the local movie house. The fact that there *is* a local movie house.

I turn off the radio, listen to the quiet. Which has its own, rich sound. Which I knew, but had forgotten. And it is good to remember.

Four

❖

I AM SITTING IN THE FAMILY ROOM IN DAVID'S RECLINER looking at the *Martha by Mail* catalogue and remembering a time when I had a long-lasting flu and David came home with a handmade quilt that he'd bought for me. He covered me with it, then lay down beside me and read me a story from a collection I'd just bought. And then he made spaghetti for him and Travis, and soup for me. That was Before. When did After start? I don't remember it starting. I only remember it having arrived. Things were bad for such a long time before he left. But I miss him. I can feel loneliness in me like circulation; as constant and as irrefutable.

I see that Martha has some very lovely hors d'oeuvres accessories. Paper leaves on which to serve cunning canapés that take about a month to make. I don't really believe that Martha herself does any of this. People say she does, but I just don't think it's true. I'll bet she lies in the bathtub and weeps and her staff does everything. I flip through pages of matelassé bedding, egg-shaped soaps, ribbon mirrors. I'll bet she's lonely as hell and no one knows. They think she's rich and happy and they don't understand how blank her slate is.

I'll bet no one even calls her, except for business. I heard she lives in Connecticut, was it Fairfield? I pick up the phone, call information, hear the automated voice ask, "What city?" "Fairfield, Connecticut," I say. "What listing?" the voice asks, and I say, "Martha Stewart." "Please hold," a real voice says, and I hang up.

The phone rings immediately and I let the machine get it, then hear Rita say, "Are you there? It's me."

I pick up the phone. "Oh, God, Rita. I thought you were Martha Stewart."

"*What?*"

"Never mind. How are you? You got my letter?"

"*Yes,* I got your *letter*. Why didn't you call me?"

"I don't know. I didn't feel like talking about it."

"Do you now?"

I say nothing.

"Well, I *never* liked him. You know that. And I'm not just saying that to make you feel better."

"Oh, don't worry, no chance of that."

"I mean, remember when you got engaged, and you showed me the ring? I thought you were crazy. I didn't like that ring. It was tasteless. Almost two carats, when we were eating dinner from cans!"

True. We did eat dinner from cans, Rita and I. We were in our first apartment, still students. We ate Hormel Chili, Franco-American Spaghetti, Dinty Moore stew—usually unheated. If we were stoned, we made do with chocolate chips.

Then one evening when I was riding the bus home from class, I met David. He asked me for a drink, told me in the smoky bar that his car was in the shop, that's why he was on the bus; normally he never rode the bus. He looked exactly like Paul Newman with brown eyes, that's what I told everyone; and everyone who met him agreed, with a kind of reluctant awe—after all, what was Newman without his eyes?

David came from a family of extraordinary wealth, but he claimed not to be affected by it; said he preferred, actually, living well below his means. With certain exceptions. His car, for instance, an antique Morgan that he loved so much for its voluptuous lines he forgave it every inconvenience. His clothes, too, that David said were no big deal, but whose labels and fabrics suggested otherwise. After making love with him the first time, I walked around the apartment for the rest of the night wearing only his pale yellow V neck, so as to fully appreciate the feel of fine cashmere. "Keep it," he'd said, yawning, when he left that night, and went home wearing a jacket over his T-shirt. Later, Rita had borrowed the sweater and spilled red wine on it, which only prompted David to buy two more—one for each of us.

"You were jealous," I tell Rita.

"I was not! I felt sorry for you, that you . . . I don't know, you stopped having fun. You started being serious all the time, trying really hard to be whatever he wanted you to be, whatever the hell that was. I honestly felt sorry for you. Everybody did! You just . . ., *lost* yourself."

I am too busy to respond to such an accusation. I am concentrating on drawing a square on my knee with my finger. The sides are not coming out even, I can tell, even though the square is invisible. I can't draw, either.

"You don't believe me?"

"Oh God, Rita, I don't know. I don't remember."

I do remember, though. I felt, marrying David, like a child handed a gift that was too big. I was convinced that I loved him, but it was a nervous love, even at the start; and there was a certain holding back on his part that seemed mean-spirited. But I was sure I could change that. His family was cold; it wasn't his fault; what he wanted more than anything was to open himself up. I would be his wife and help him. Over the years, I looked for ways into him, for an essential kind of access; and I failed at finding it again and again.

"So what are your plans?" Rita asks.

I look out the kitchen window. Puffy clouds like the kind Travis used to draw, a deep blue sky. It's beautiful outside. The earth turns. Yesterday, I made a list that said: *Clear yard of debris. Get gas. Return calls.* I might as well have added: *Eat. Breathe.*

"I don't really have any plans," I say. "Plans are too hard. All I've done so far is to spend a whole bunch of money."

"Well, good. That's a start. What'd you buy, under-wear? That's what my friend Eileen did. The day her hus-band left—for a fucking dental hygienist who'd given *both* of them these weird *gum* massages—she went to Victoria's Secret and spent five hundred dollars in about fifteen minutes. She got matching everything. And a whole bunch of dirty stuff. Lewinsky thongs, garter belts . . ."

"I went to Tiffany's. I got china. And silver." I won't mention the bracelet. No need to get into *that*.

"You're kidding!"

"No."

"You don't like that stuff."

"Well, I never did before, but now I do. I just want . . . something different. I'm going to live another way. I have to live another way. I mean, even things like learning not to be afraid of the dark. Did you know I'm afraid of the dark? I lie awake at night now, wondering who's in the basement getting ready to come upstairs and murder me and Travis. I keep a fish knife under my bed."

"A *fish* knife?"

"Well, I'd never used it. I figured I might as well use it. It's very nice. Pearl-handled."

"I'm sure the killer will appreciate that."

"That would be a pretty nice change, being appreciated." All the things I really want to tell Rita are stuck in my throat. I cannot say them, it's too embarrassing. *I sat in the middle of the living-room floor and howled like a dog, Rita. I've been contemplating "accidental" death. I bought a book on self-esteem, and when the author said to make a list of what I liked about myself, I couldn't do it. I could not write down one thing. After two days, I made one that kind of copied the suggested list, then hid it in my underwear drawer, then burned it. I can't think straight; my head is full of cobwebs. I have to concentrate really hard to open a can of soup.*

Gently, Rita says, "Sam, why don't you get away for a while? Come out here. I'll take time off from work, I'll take care of you."

Why don't I visit Rita? She lives in a beautiful house in Mill Valley, in Marin County. I could fly out to San Francisco tonight, lie around in the hammock in Rita's beautiful backyard tomorrow, staring at the gently rounded hills, at the ocean glittering in the distance. We could eat avocado and tomato and sprout sandwiches, take long walks, make bouquets of the extraordinary wildflowers that grow everywhere. Rita's husband, Lawrence, is a humanities professor, gray-eyed and bearded and calm. He casts coins for the I Ching. He is an inventive chef, and he cooks at least twice a week. He would leave us alone when we needed to be left alone, join us when we wanted him to.

Rita always puts fresh flowers in my room, as well as a huge box of chocolates and a *National Enquirer*. She plays the music she and I used to listen to when we were roommates: the Temptations, Janis, Odetta. We talk for hours, laugh until we cry.

Finally, though, I say, "I can't come out there. Travis is in school. I can't just pull him out. And I don't want to leave him with David."

"Leave him with your mother, then. She loves to try to wreck him."

"I think I need to hang around. I mean, this is hard for him, too."

"Oh, I know. I'm sorry. I don't mean to underestimate any of this. I really don't. How is Travis, anyway?"

"Mostly not talking. I think he thinks it's just a big fight."

"Is it?"

"No. It's been coming for a long time. I don't think he ever loved me. It's sort of astonishing, isn't it?" I start to cry. Again.

"Oh, honey," Rita says. "I know how this hurts. I'm so sorry. I wish I could be there now, I'd do something."

"I know you would. It would be something wonderful, too. What would it be?"

"Well, I would . . . I have no idea, actually."

I laugh, blow my nose. "So you always thought he was a jerk, huh?"

"I really did."

"Did you talk behind his back?"

"Constantly."

"I hope you mentioned what a terrible dancer he was. Absolutely no sense of rhythm. Not that he knew that."

"We covered that, I'm sure. As well as that reptilian gesture he made whenever he cleared his throat, sticking his chin out that way. And Sam, I know you feel awful now, but I think, in the end, you'll be so much better off without him. You used to wear mascara to *bed*."

"Well."

"And when you had Travis, you were embarrassed that David saw the umbilical cord."

Oh God, I'd forgotten that. But it's true. I'd felt bad about how ugly it was.

I hear the clock chime three. "I've got to go, Rita. Travis will be home soon."

"Call me tonight."

"What for?"

"I need support, okay?"

Upstairs, I wash my face, reapply some eyeliner. Then I take off all my clothes and stare at my naked self in the bathroom mirror. I turn to the side. Good breasts. But the beginning of dimpling at the tops of my thighs. And there is my stupid, flabby stomach. I wonder at what age pubic hair turns gray. I don't see how people who were married for a long time can ever take their clothes off in front of another person. Another lover. How can there ever be another lover? The hands would be wrong. The face. The smell. You'd open your eyes from a kiss and . . . what? No map.

I put my clothes back on. Then I head downstairs to make some peanut-butter cookies for Travis. Also chocolate chip.

It's Friday, the weekend looming ahead. Tonight we're going out to dinner, to an Italian place on Newbury Street that has no business charging what it does. We'll valet park. We'll get appetizers before our entrées and dessert after them. "To drink?" the waiter will say, and I will consult the wine list, pick by price.

"I DON'T WANT an appetizer," Travis says. He is trying to keep his voice low, but he is agitated. We are seated at the restaurant after having been shown to our table with a certain restrained condescension. It is early, five-thirty; no other customers have the poor taste to be here. Most of the waiters sit in a small, white-coated group at a table in the back of the room, lazily gossiping, laughing, drinking what looks like ice water with lemon slices in it.

"I just want spaghetti with butter and cheese."

"Yes, well, you can have that," I tell him. "But wouldn't you like to start with something else?"

"Start what?"

"Start your dinner, honey."

"*Spaghetti* is my dinner."

"Yes, but you can have an appetizer as well. You can have both. Come on, you know that."

"Fine." He snaps his menu closed, slumps back in his chair. He yanks at his tie, loosening it.

"So!" I say. "What will it be? You can have anything you want."

"I don't care. You're the one who wants it. You pick."

I straighten in my chair, smile at the approaching waiter. He is so elegantly gay I feel ashamed of myself, of my predictable domestic status. Breeder. Divorced. Knowledge of nightlife and art scene nil.

The waiter stands before me, raises an eyebrow. "Have we decided?"

Antipasto? I'm thinking, a little panicked. *Shrimp in lime vinaigrette?* And then, because Travis is right, this is all only exhausting, I say, "Spaghetti with butter and grated cheese for my son, please. And for me, too. Don't be stingy with that Parmesan, either. Two Cokes, no ice. Four cannoli. And the check."

"All right," the waiter says, and accompanies the snappy motion of his pen sliding back into his breast pocket with a tight smile.

"All *right*!" Travis yells, and sits up straighter.

"Travis?"

He looks up at me, fearful, I know, of being told he's talking too loud.

"Why don't you take off that tie?" I slip my heels off, lean back in my chair.

Travis removes his tie, coils it into a neat arrangement at the side of his plate. Beside it, I lay my belt.

Hours later, after Travis and I watch *Star Wars* twice, he falls into bed. I wash up and go into my bedroom, intent on reading one of the new books I bought the other day. I turn back the bedclothes and then, just like that, all the good feeling I've built up today seems to drain out of the soles of my feet. I stand there for a while. And then I get down on my knees, and whisper, *Help me* into my folded hands.

Five

On Monday morning, right after Travis leaves for school, the phone rings. When I answer it, I hear an extremely irritated voice say, "What the hell are you doing, Sam?"

"Oh. Hello, David."

"What are you *do*ing?"

"I'm standing here, David. I'm standing here talking on the phone. What are you doing? Where are you?"

"At work."

Not in his car in the driveway, then, calling to see if I'll take him back.

"I just had a conversation with John Hurley at the bank. Very interesting. It appears that a large check was written to Tiffany's last week. By you."

"That's right. I needed some dishes."

"Uh-huh. Well, I suppose this is one way for you to get back at me. Rather unimaginative, I must say."

"I suppose you must. Not nearly as original as packing a bag and moving to a hotel."

"Sam, I'm calling to tell you I've transferred most of the money into another account. I'm sorry, but you really leave me no choice."

He . . . ?

Oh, God.

Well, fine, then. *Fine.* What should I have for breakfast?

"I'll provide adequately for Travis. And for you as well. But not so adequately that you can buy twelve thousand dollars' worth of merchandise at Tiffany's on a random Thursday afternoon."

Shredded Wheat with strawberries? Eggs?

"Sam?"

"Yes?"

"Are you listening to me? Do you understand?"

I hang up. Then lift the receiver and hang up again, harder. Then take the phone off the cradle, lay it on the kitchen table.

I'll get a job. I'll make my own damn money. I'll rent out David's study, and maybe the basement, too. That will do nicely to help to pay the mortgage. I'll keep the house, not sell it, as David said we must. I live here. Travis lives here. And I will stay here. I will, in fact, do whatever I want to do. Use the chain saw in the toolshed, which David said was too dangerous. Wear purple eye shadow, which David said was too tacky.

As for now, I'll go out and take a long walk.

I start for the door, then look at the phone, lying on the table. *We tried to reach you, Mrs. Morrow. But your line was busy. The principal signed the release form for the surgery.*

I put the phone back in the cradle, take a step, and hear it ring. I pick it up. "I *heard* you."

"Heard what?" my mother asks.

"Oh. Ma. I thought you were David. He just called."

"And?"

"He needed to talk about finances. Nothing, really."

"Well, speaking of finances, I found a coupon for forty percent off a permanent. Are you interested?"

"I don't want a perm."

"I think it might look very nice."

"You use it, Ma."

"I have a perm!"

"Well, I'll bet one of your friends can use it."

"That's a thought. You remember Angie Ryan? I'll give it to her, she needs a lift. Her husband should be institutionalized. Do you know what he did to that poor woman last week?"

Oh, well. I pull out a kitchen chair. Sit down.

TRAVIS IS UPSTAIRS doing homework, and I am sitting at the kitchen table, making a list.

1. CALL DAVID TO COME AND GET ALL HIS SHIT, I write. Then, fearing Travis will see it, I erase SHIT and substitute THINGS. In parentheses I add, SO HE WILL HAVE WHAT HE NEEDS.

Next I write: 2. POST SIGN IN FRANCO'S SUPER-MARKET FOR ROOMMATE(S?).

Then, 3. JOB.

A job doing what? I imagine filling out the application. *Last job?* Girl singer in rock band. *References?* "Roach" Davis, lead guitarist.

I wonder whatever happened to him. He might have made a career out of being a studio musician; he was really good. He could roll joints with one hand, and he taught me how, too. Now, there's something useful I might put on my application.

Oh, what can I do?

What do I want to do?

I rest my head on my arms, close my eyes, recall something that happened many years ago. When I was a first-grader, I once went to the bank with my mother. Outside, sitting against the wall on a red, worn blanket, was a man with legs that ended somewhere around his knees.

His tan khaki pants were folded neatly beneath his stumps, and the matter-of-factness of this horrified me. The man held a cigar box out, rattled the change inside it, and smiled up at us, squinting against the bright sun. Then he tipped his straw hat and asked, "Can you help me out, ladies? Spare a little change?" I burst into tears so loud and heartfelt my mother immediately pulled me away, brought me back to the car, and rolled up the windows. "Shhhhh, it's all *right*," she said, dabbing at my face with a hankie and looking nervously about. And I said, no, it *wasn't* all right, the man didn't have any *legs*, he couldn't even stand *up*. My mother said well, yes, that was right, but the man was here all the time, and he was happy, really, he *liked* sitting outside the bank and collecting money. This made me cry all the harder, until, exasperated, my mother finally pressed a dollar bill in my hand and told me to give it to the man, but to be sure not to touch him. I wiped my reddened face on the hem of my dress, then walked slowly over to give the man the money. "*Thank* you, little lady," he said, and I told him he was welcome. And then I did touch him, I reached out and touched his arm and he put his hand over my hand and that was when I stopped hurting.

I sit up. Maybe I can get a job in the nursing home a few blocks away. Every time I pass it, I look in the window to watch bits of activity: a woman dressed in a pastel sweat suit being pushed in a wheelchair down the hall; a circle of people in what looks to be a community room, singing. I've always had the urge to go in there and offer something. Maybe I will now. "I don't really have any job experience," I imagine saying. "But I really like old people."

The salary doesn't have to be much, if I can find roommates. The important thing is that I do something that's

meaningful to me, that's the truth for me. I'm going to
start telling the truth. A woman I know once made a
New Year's resolution to tell the truth, and I remember
thinking how extraordinary—and how difficult—that
would be. You make such a resolution and no matter
what someone asks you, you have to answer honestly.
Think of it!

"I'm working in a nursing home," I say aloud, trying
it out.

The phone rings and I answer it distractedly. A man
clears his throat, then says, "Yes. I'm looking for Sam
Reynolds." *Reynolds*. My maiden name. It must be a
high school reunion, I think, and answer with some ex-
citement that yes, this is Sam. I always loved Greg Mul-
vaney, the pitcher on our baseball team: dark, Italian,
dimples. I never told him. Maybe he's divorced now, too.
A slow dance, a tentative confession . . . perhaps on both
of our parts. Who knows what could happen? I push the
bowl of potato chips I've been eating away from me.

But then the man says, "I'm Stuart Gardner. Your
mother gave me your number."

". . . Oh?"

"She told me you might be willing to meet me. Say,
for a drink tonight? She thought we'd have a lot in
common."

"Did she."

"Yes, she did. For one thing—"

"What was your name?"

"Stuart. Stuart Gardner. Like the museum."

"Uh-huh. Well, you know, I really think it's a little
soon, Stuart. My husband—did my mother tell you?"

"Yes, I'm very sorry. She said he'd died over a year ago,
though, and she thought you might be ready for . . . just a
drink, is all I'm talking about. Or coffee, whatever."

"I'm sorry, Stuart. I really don't think so."

He sighs, a petulant sound that makes me sure I wouldn't like him anyway, then asks, "Well, would you at least be willing to take my number?"

"Oh, sure."

"You have a pencil?"

I do, of course, but I do not pick it up. "Yes, I have one."

"It's six-four-nine . . ."

I repeat the numbers back slowly, then say, "Okay!"

"I really think we'd get along," Stuart says. "Your mother's told me a lot about you."

"Maybe after a while. I'll call you when I'm ready. But I'm still having flashbacks, you know. I still see his face when I, you know, shot him."

"You . . . ?"

"Just kidding."

Silence.

I hang up, realize I have broken my vow to tell the truth already. But I will get back on track right now. I pick up the phone, punch in my mother's number. When Veronica answers with her usual happy and expectant "Yes, *hello*?" I yell, "What is the *matter* with you?"

"Sam! Is that you?"

"Don't get me a date! With anyone! Ever!"

"Oh, did Stuart call you? He's the nicest man. You'll just love him."

"Wait a minute. *Wait* a minute! I just said, don't *do* this! And you're acting like I'm thrilled, like I just made plans for a rendezvous in Paris!"

Veronica chuckles. "Well, not a *ren*dezvous. Not even a date. Just a drink, sweetheart. That way, you find out a little about each other. *Then* you date. Dinner, maybe a movie, although you can't really talk in a movie, I never did understand going to a movie on a first date. But dinner in a nice, oh, say, French restaurant, flowers on the table, not *too* expensive, but something that—"

I lean against the wall, instantly exhausted. But I manage to say, "Ma. Listen to me. If anyone else calls me, I will hang up on them. I swear I will. I will just hang up."

Silence.

"Do you hear me?"

"Sam, you sound awfully blue. I'm worried about you."

"I will hang up!"

"Well, fine, then. You just mope all you want to. Little Miss Blue. Some people revel in their misery. Some people just love to be unhappy."

"I need to find my own way, Mother."

"Well, good for you. You want to weep and gnash your teeth and carry on, go right ahead. Have a good time. That's really great for Travis, too."

"I am not gnashing my teeth. I'm getting a job. And roommates."

"*Roommates?*"

"Yes."

"You're going to open your house to *strangers*? Oh, Lord."

I hang up, refill the potato-chip bowl, and do not answer the phone when it rings again. I sit down with my list, add, LET MACHINE TAKE ALL CALLS.

Six

I AM AT FRANCO'S, THE SMALL NEIGHBORHOOD GRO-
cery store walking distance from my house. It's more expensive, but less overwhelming than the supermarket,
and there are small touches that offer comfort everywhere. Free coffee. A recipe-exchange board. The soft
sounds of classical music in the background, with no
overly excited voice breaking in to describe unbelievable
savings on London broil. The smell of turkey roasting in
the back room.

The aisles are named for nearby streets, and their
signs are hand painted in curly black script. Polite, high
school–aged boys with neatly combed hair and clear com-
plexions bag the groceries and, unless refused, bring them
out to the car, no tipping allowed. This, of course, only
makes customers more anxious to tip. But the boys stead-
fastly turn the money down, and on their way back into
the store, they collect any stray carts and arrange them in a
neat line outside the door. I can't imagine where they find
these young men. When they go home at night, it must be
to the 1950s.

The older people who work in the store are department managers. They are vigilant, restacking pyramids
of tomatoes, straightening cartons of cottage cheese, stirring up the pasta salad at the deli counter. I like to be

checked out by Marie, the cashier who's worked at Franco's for thirty-one years, and I wait in line for her now, ignoring the other cashier whose register is free. I want to ask Marie where on the community bulletin board I should pin my sign; some spots might be better than others. I've seen ads for places for rent before, stuck between ads for free cats, baby-sitting, piano lessons, carpenters willing to do small jobs. I've carefully printed my message on an index card:

ROOMMATE WANTED

Large bedroom for rent in very nice house with single woman and eleven-year-old son. No smoking. Pets or kids okay. Must be employed and responsible. $500/mo.

It occurred to me, writing it, that it didn't say enough. But I didn't know how to add more. *Please don't be one of those types who never wears deodorant,* I couldn't say that. *Please become my friend, I need a friend.* I couldn't say that either. *No hospitalizations for psychosis,* Rita had suggested. *Neurotics okay.*

Well, I'll see who calls, that's all; then interview them, take it from there. I trust my intuition. I know about people. Except for David. *Please don't be like David.*

"Hey! Wake up," Marie says, reaching over to pull my cart forward.

I smile, begin unloading my few groceries.

"What's for dinner?" Marie asks, looking over her half glasses to see what I've selected. Then, "What's wrong?"

"Oh, it's just . . . I need to post a sign, Marie. Where's a good spot on the board?"

"What are you selling?"

"I'm renting a room. In my house."

"Really?"

"Yes, I need . . . a roommate." The word is ridiculous. I am forty-two years old.

Marie hands me my change, tells the other check-out clerk that she'll be right back. "Come with me," she says, and leads me into the back room. Cases of soda are piled high; time cards are lined up on a rack on the wall. *Get a job.*

"What's going on, hon?" she asks.

I shrug, sit down on a box full of seltzer bottles.

"You and your husband split up or something?"

I nod.

"Well, I'll be damned." Marie sighs, leans back against the time clock, crosses her arms over her blue cotton smock. "Franco's" is gaily embroidered over one breast; over the other she wears her name tag, pinned, as usual, at an odd angle. She doesn't need a name tag, anyway. Everybody knows her; she is everyone's surrogate something. She is in her late fifties, overweight in the deeply comforting way. She has compassionate blue eyes, salt-and-pepper hair, beautiful skin that she has told me she owes to mayonnaise masks. I've been exchanging mindless pleasantries with her for years: comments on the weather, criticism of the Red Sox, a shared interest in Travis's growth. Marie was the first person outside the immediate family to hold Travis; I brought him to the store when he was three weeks old.

"When did this all happen?" Marie asks.

"A couple of weeks ago. I'm keeping the house, but I'll need some help with the mortgage payment. So I thought I'd advertise for a roommate."

"Oh, boy. I don't know."

"Is there any place on the board that people look at more than other places?"

She frowns. "Are you sure about this? You could get a real nut."

"Well, I don't know what else to do. I can't afford it by myself."

"Wait a minute!" Marie says. "I've got a prospect for you. My mother needs a place."

"Your mother!"

"Her rent's going up again. She can't afford her own apartment anymore, but she doesn't want to live with me—wants to keep her independence. She's an awfully nice woman, Sam, real quiet, tidy, loves children. And you know all those great recipes I gave you? They're hers."

A grandmother. Probably a real one, too, not one like my mother is to Travis. Someone who wears pearl studs and pastel dresses that reach mid-calf, rather than gold stretch pants with tight sweaters and multiple necklaces. It could work, why not? And if I can rent out the basement, too, I wouldn't have to worry so much about the salary at any job I take.

I tear a piece of paper from my grocery bag. "Here's my number. Have her call me. I'd love to meet her."

"There is one thing . . ."

"Yes?" *Incontinence.*

"She has a boyfriend. They're . . . close."

"Oh! Well, one of us might as well have one."

I shoulder my purse, stand. "Thanks, Marie."

She nods, sad for me. Although, I realize, I'm not sad for myself. Not at the moment. The relief makes me feel light. Maybe I really am lighter. Grief has a catabolic effect. That must make you lose weight. In the car, I check my face in the rearview mirror. It looks exactly the same. And then, just like that, I am sad again. I start the car, turn on the radio, hear *What becomes of a broken heart?* Good question.

"THIS IS SUCH a crazy time," I tell Rita. "One minute I feel awful, and then I feel kind of . . . *ecstatic.*"

"Yeah, that's what everybody says." She is making dinner; I hear water running, the muted clanging of pots and pans. "That you just ride this emotional roller coaster."

"Exactly. The other night, I was lying in the bathtub crying. Today I feel like the day I got married is the day the lights went out. That I'm lucky to be rid of him."

"You are."

"What are you making?"

"Chicken," Rita says. "What else does anyone eat anymore? Imagine how the hens feel bringing their children into the world."

"Listen, I think I found a roommate."

A beat, and then Rita says, "You *can't* have, already! You have to take some time, Sam. You have to be careful!"

"It's a seventy-eight-year-old woman, for God's sake. I know her daughter."

"What does Travis think about that?"

"Well, I haven't told him. He knows we're going to be getting a roommate, but he doesn't know who, or when. I want to make sure she's really moving in before I tell him about her."

Rita sighs. "You want to live with an old lady. Now, there's a major improvement. Maybe you can go play Bingo together, wear each other's shawls. That's it, I'm coming out there. You need me."

"I don't think it's such a bad idea. She likes to cook, for one thing. And I want to rent out the basement, too. I'll get someone more my age for down there. Or someone much younger, maybe a twenty-year-old. A biker, how's that?"

I hear the doorbell and say, "She's here—the woman! She's here to meet me."

"At night? She goes out at night?"

"I've got to go."

"Be *careful*!"

"Of an old woman?"

"Remember Bette Davis? *Baby Jane?*"

"I'll call you later." I hang up, push my hair back from my face, and go to the door.

But it is not the woman at the door; it is David, ringing the bell to be sure I understand that he no longer lives here, I suppose. "He wanted to come home," David says. He looks over his shoulder at Travis, moving slowly up the sidewalk.

"You were supposed to keep him till bedtime!"

"He wanted to come home, Sam, what do you want me to do? Why does he have to be gone, anyway? What are *you* doing?"

Travis comes in, drops his book bag on the hall floor, heads for the kitchen. "What's to eat?"

"What happened?" I ask David.

He shrugs. "He's tired, I think. Has he been sleeping? Have you been putting him to bed on time?"

"What's to *eat*?" Travis yells.

"You were supposed to eat with *Dad*," I yell back. "I didn't make anything! I don't *have* anything!"

Travis comes back into the hallway. "You don't have *anything*?"

I look at David, see the same question in his eyes. Outside, I see an older model gray Oldsmobile pull under the streetlight. A man gets out, dressed in a dark suit and hat, and goes around to open the door for an older woman. She takes a long look at the house, reaching behind herself to straighten the back of her dress.

"You and Travis have to leave," I tell David quietly. "Right now."

He turns to watch the couple coming up the walk. "Who's that?"

"I'm interviewing a roommate."

"Are you kidding?" He looks again.

I'm not sure, suddenly, of anything. But with an authority that surprises me, I say, "Take Travis out for dinner. Right now. He was supposed to eat with you."

"I told you, he doesn't want to go!"

"Take him anyway."

From behind me, I hear Travis say, "That's our roommate? Old people?"

I take him gently by the arm. "It's the woman I'll be talking to. You go and get some dinner with Dad. I'll talk to you when you get home, I'll tell you all about it. Don't worry about a thing." I push him out the door with David, then straighten to wave to the couple. The woman is carrying a black patent leather pocketbook by the handle, using both hands. She is smiling. Her boyfriend cradles her elbow, guides her tenderly along. He has a white mustache, neatly trimmed, and he is wearing a bow tie. This woman can move in tonight. They both can.

THE PHONE RINGS just after I've gone to sleep. I squint to see the numbers on the clock. Eleven-thirty.

"You told her she could move in, didn't you?" Rita asks, when I pick up the receiver.

"Oh, hi. I was sleeping."

"You did, didn't you?"

"Yes, I did."

"Great."

"It is great. You'd like her."

"I'm sure I would. I'm also sure I wouldn't want to live with her."

"Why not? What is this prejudice you have against older people? I never knew this about you." I get out of bed, quietly close the bedroom door.

"I'm not prejudiced. I just think you should think a little more about who you want to *live* with, I mean, didn't the last experience teach you anything?"

"She'll be fine. She has a wonderful boyfriend, this old, refined-looking gentleman who just . . . he is so vigilant, so attentive. We had tea together. We had a nice time. She's moving in next week. Tomorrow I'm getting all David's stuff moved out."

"To where?"

"Oh, he found a condo already. I think he'd been looking for a while."

"Jesus."

"It's okay."

"No, it isn't."

"Listen, Rita, I'm going back to sleep. We can fight tomorrow."

I hang up, then go to Travis's room. He's asleep, the phone didn't wake him. That's good—he had a rough night. He didn't understand why he had to leave with David when he wanted to stay home. He didn't understand why we really are getting a roommate, despite my careful explanations.

I stand beside him, my arms wrapped around myself, then reach down to pull the covers up to his shoulders. He stirs slightly, resettles himself. I kiss the top of his head, then go to sit in the chair in the corner of his room. I can smell him in the air. It is such a fine smell, faintly like earth, but saltier. I pick up one of his stuffed animals, an ancient bear, and hold it on my lap. Its size is close to the size Travis was when I first began reading out loud to him—I can rest my chin on the top of the bear's head, just as I used to do with Travis.

I don't hold Travis anymore, of course—not to read to him, or for any other reason, either. I wish I'd known that the last time was going to *be* the last time. But of course that information would have been as painful as this moment. When Travis had gotten his first haircut, after all, the barber had handed me his handkerchief with a smile, then a box of tissues, with no smile.

I lean my head back, close my eyes. I am so deeply tired. And I am afraid. The truth is, I have no idea what I'm doing. It's not fair that my son has a mother like this. His mother should know what she's doing.

Seven

LATE WEDNESDAY AFTERNOON, A SMALL MOVING TRUCK pulls up to the curb. *Promove.* Sounds like someone David might hire. Two men who look as though they must be father and son get out of the truck, talk to each other before they start for the door. I wonder what they're saying. *Remember—this is a divorce situation, here. We'll have to be careful. Don't say anything to the Mrs.—she might start bawling.*

I open the door, stand waiting on the porch. "Hi!" I say. *Oh, God.*

"Mrs. Morrow?" the older man says.

"Yes!"

"We're here to pick up a few of Mr. Morrow's things?"

"Yes!" I step out of the way to let them in. "The study is the last room on the right, upstairs. The master is to the left—you'll find all his clothes at one end of the closet."

"This won't take too long," the man says, and something in the kind tone of his voice reaches my knees. I go into the kitchen, where I will find something to do. I can't watch them. *We'd gotten ham and cheese subs for lunch. While we sat on the empty living-room floor and watched the moving men carry his desk upstairs, David put his*

*Coke bottle up to mine for a toast. "I love this house," he
said. "We're never moving."*

I organize pots and pans, wipe out cupboards, line up
spice bottles. When I hear the man call out, "All set!" I
come into the living room.

"All set," he says, again, quietly. Beside him, his son
frankly stares at me, three fingers on his hip, football-
player style.

"So, if you could just sign here."

"Oh, sure." I take the man's ballpoint pen—it's
greasy—and start to sign my name. And then I drop the
pen onto the clipboard and put my hands to my face.

"Oh, boy," the man says. And then, "I'm awful sorry,
Miss."

I stop crying, pick up the pen, sign my name. Say
thank you. Watch them drive away. Go upstairs and regard the empty room. *David, we can't do it in here!
Shhhhh! Take off your clothes, we'll be so quiet we won't
hear us.*

I sit in the middle of the floor and rock like an autistic.
There is comfort in it. In the corner, I see a paper clip, and
I pick it up and hold it. Then I put it in my pocket. And
then I go to the bedroom, look in the closet. Yup. They
got it all.

I sit on the edge of the bed, stare at the wall. Then I
take the paper clip out of my pocket and put it in the top
drawer of the nightstand.

Now. Now I'll call Karen Wheeler to tell her it's safe
for Travis to come home, and that he can bring Ben, too,
if he wants. And I know what Karen will say. She'll say
Oh, well, why doesn't Travis just stay here for a while?
Because she won't want Ben here. Because what if it's
contagious?

Ben answers the phone when I call. "Hey, Ben," I say.

"It's Travis's mom. I just wanted to tell you that Travis can come home anytime. And you can come, too, if you want. Stay for dinner?"

"Oh, okay. Hold on a second." He puts the phone down and I hear him say, "Hey, T. Want to go over to your house? Your mom says it's okay."

Silence. And then Ben comes back to the phone. "He says we'll just stay here. Okay?"

". . . Sure. Can I speak to him, though?"

Another moment, and then Ben comes back to the phone again. "Mrs. Morrow?"

"Yes?"

"He's doing something now. He says he'll see you later."

"Oh. All right. Thank you, Ben."

"It's just . . . We're playing this computer game. He's at the hard part."

He's a sweet kid, Ben. He forgives me.

WHEN TRAVIS COMES home, he asks if the study is completely empty. "Yes," I say. "Would you like to see it?"

"Why would I want to see an empty room?"

But after we've gone to bed, I hear his door open and I know exactly where he's going. And I know he needs to be alone, going there. My body lies in bed while my mind stands beside him, apologizing, apologizing, apologizing.

Eight

MARIE IS THE FIRST TO ARRIVE, READY TO HELP HER mother move in. It is Saturday morning, a crisp and clear late October day, the sky a rare dark blue. When I went out for the paper, I stood shivering in the driveway for a while, looking up appreciatively until I felt dizzy. Then I came back inside to make banana bread. It's almost a reflex—every time I feel happy, I need to make something to eat. Also every time I feel sad.

So there is the rich smell of banana bread in the air now, as well as freshly brewed coffee; and Marie sniffs deeply as she takes off her coat. "Smells good!" she tells me. Then, looking around, "Say, this is a nice house! Maybe I'll move in, too. You know, leave the old man. He probably wouldn't notice anyway."

Really? I almost ask. I show Marie the rest of the house, including the study where her mother will be living. "Perfect," Marie says. And then, looking at me, "You okay?"

"Yeah!"

"Really?"

"Well . . . Yes. Yes. Thank you."

And then the Ryder truck arrives, a man driving it who's been hired to help carry stuff in. There wasn't much, Lydia had assured me: some bedroom furniture, a few kitchen things, linens. The apartment she lived in before had been mostly furnished.

I stand at the window and watch the man climb out of the truck, note with satisfaction that he is huge. I won't need to help much. He opens the back doors of the truck and pulls out a brass headboard, which glints magnificently in the sun.

"Boy, that bed is old," Marie says, sipping coffee and standing beside me. "My mother was born in it. And her mother."

I see a woman in the bed with wavy, dark hair loosened about her head, perspiring, another woman wearing a long skirt and a white blouse with rolled-up sleeves, standing by to wipe her face with a soft, folded cloth, to speak quietly into her ear, a woman who has had children herself and thus communicates in a higher language.

When I was in labor, David sat beside me eating the dinner the hospital provided and complaining that it was cold. I turned the call light on for the nurse, who, upon entering, asked, "Need something for pain, hon?"

"No, thank you," I said. And then, pointing to David's tray, "It's cold."

"Oh," she said. "Okay. I'll take care of it right away." She took David's tray from him, said in a low voice to me, "First things first, right?" *Oh, no, you don't know him,* I'd wanted to say. But maybe she did.

I see the moving man coming up the walk and I go to the door to meet him. He is probably well over six foot three, and his weight is considerable. He is fat, is the plain truth, and yet I find him extremely pleasant to look at. It has to do with his beautiful black hair, cut in an appealingly shaggy way. And his brown eyes, they're nice too—golden, almost. He is wearing faded blue jeans, a white shirt with the sleeves rolled up, black suspenders, and red high-top sneakers; no coat. He smells faintly of soap.

"Aren't you cold?" I ask.

"Nope." He smiles at me. Nice teeth.

I smile back. Lean against the doorjamb, arms crossed.

"Did you want me to tell him where to put it, Sam?" Marie asks.

"Oh! I'm sorry," I say. "It's up—well, here, let me show you." I lead him up the staircase, conscious of my backside as I always am, leading one damn workman or another upstairs or downstairs. It doesn't matter who they are: meter man, furnace-repair man, furniture-delivery man: every time I walk in front of them, I can feel them judging my ass. Even if they're not. But probably they are.

I take him to the study. "This is it." I move to the window and open the shade. The room fills with light, and, inexplicably, this fills me with a kind of optimism and pride.

The man leans the bed frame gently against the wall, then extends his hand. "My name is King."

I laugh. "It is?"

"Honest to God. My parents were . . . different."

"Well," I say. "I'm sorry for laughing. It's just, you know . . . Graceland. I'm Sam."

"So you'll be Lydia's roommate?"

"Yes. You know her? Lydia?"

"Just met her. Her and her boyfriend, nice people. They have a lot of class. Something you don't see much of anymore." He motions for me to go ahead of him out of the room. "She doesn't have much stuff. This won't take long."

"I made some banana bread, and there's coffee," I say. I agree with what he just said about Lydia. Therefore, I will feed him.

Downstairs, I see that Lydia has arrived. She is taking her coat off, adjusting her open-weave cardigan sweater, asking her daughter where the closet is again, and Marie is saying she's not sure, either.

"I'll hang that up," I say, taking her coat, and then, shyly, "Hello. Welcome."

Lydia smiles, takes my hand between her own. Her hands are warm, strong; not dry and fragile feeling, as I had thought they would be. My hands, however, reflect my nervousness—I know they're ice-cold. I lead the women into the kitchen, set out cups and plates for them, slice the banana bread.

After we sit down, Lydia pushes a small package toward me. "For you," she says. And then, when I start to protest, she says, "It's nothing. Very small." I unwrap crystal salt and pepper shakers, start to say thank you when I am interrupted by a high-pitched "Yoo-hoo!" At first I'm confused, thinking the moving man has an awfully high voice, but then there is my mother, coming into the kitchen. She is wearing a lavender work-out suit, and her coat is open, car keys in her hand.

"Ma!"

"Well, you never answer the phone. I was on my way back from my aerobics class—" She looks pointedly at Marie and Lydia.

"Lydia, please meet my mother, Veronica Reynolds. Mom, this is Lydia Fitch, my new roommate; and this is her daughter, Marie Howard. It's moving day—I guess you saw the truck. . . ."

Veronica comes to the table to shake both women's hands. Her bracelets jangle busily. "Very nice to meet you, what a surprise." She doesn't say *surprise* like it's a surprise. She says it like it's a dirty trick.

"Banana bread?" Lydia asks, offering her own untouched plate, and Veronica hastily declines. "I'm on my way home, really, just dropped in to see how my daughter's doing. But apparently she's doing just fine, isn't she, got two roommates already!"

"Just one," Marie says.

"Pardon?"

"Just one, I'm not moving in. I'm just here to help my mother get settled."

"I see. Where's Travis?"

"Shopping," I say. "He went to the mall with Billy Silverman and his mother to find some pants he *must* have. All the rage."

"You let him buy his own clothes now?"

"I have for some time."

"Uh-huh. Well! Something *else* I didn't know." She looks at Lydia. "Funny, isn't it, how you can not know so much about those you're closest to? Okay, I'd better be going, I don't want to stay too long. Not even invited in the first place, of course."

"Ma. You're welcome to stay as long as you like. I'm sure you know that."

"Oh no. Really, I can't. A lot to do, for tonight. I'm having a man over for dinner. I thought, well, why not lobster, something sort of elegant? And I just found something out about lobster, too. A woman at the gym told me if you slice open their claws after they're cooked and hold them upside down over the sink, the water will run right out. Then there's no need for bibs covering up your cleavage."

A polite silence at the table. Then Veronica tells Lydia, "Well. I hope you'll be very happy here." She turns to me. "Want to walk me to the car?"

At the door, we meet King, carrying an armload of clothes and a pole lamp. He nods, smiling, and my mother pulls back to let him pass. "Well!" she says, after we get outside. "Don't get *him* mad at you! A few pounds getting a free ride there!"

"He's quite nice, really."

She climbs into her car, pulls down the visor to check herself in the mirror. "I wonder something," she says.

"What?"

She adjusts her bangs, leans in closer to the mirror, wipes away a smudge of eyeliner. "I just wonder if you could give me one reason why I couldn't have lived here with you instead of a total stranger. Who's *old*."

Let's see, I think. *One* reason?

She looks at me. "I mean, your own mother. I just wonder what you could have been thinking that you wouldn't ask me first."

"Oh, Ma, this all came about accidentally, all of a sudden. I didn't plan it. Besides, I don't know if it's such a good idea for mothers and daughters to live together after a certain age. Do you, really? I mean, if you need money—"

"I certainly *don't* need your money! Have I ever asked you for money? Ever? Even once?"

"Well, then, I'm sorry if you feel—"

Veronica puts her hand on my arm, squeezes it. "Oh, it's all right. I understand. You're confused right now, honey, doing things on the spur of the moment that you probably don't understand yourself. You didn't think to ask me. You probably thought I wouldn't want to live with you and Travis. Oh now, darling, of course I would. But not quite yet. Maybe a few years from now, all right?"

I straighten, stand silently. What is it that I feel so often around my mother? Amazement? Confusion? Is it anger?

"You know, if I did live here . . . I've always thought a little chintz in that family room is all you need. That's what I'd do. Re-cover the sofa."

"Right."

My mother turns the key in the ignition. Engelbert Humperdinck blasts out a plea for forgiveness, not having known it would end this way. Veronica respectfully turns him down. "Call me, later. There's someone I want you to meet. This one you'll really like."

"Ma—"

She flutters her fingers. "I'll talk to you soon." Then she turns the radio back up and pulls away, her right blinker gaily flashing, as it usually is. I head back for the house, irritated at the fact that my mother is right. I am confused.

I AM DREAMING that someone is shaking my shoulder. And then I realize that someone *is* shaking my shoulder. "What," I say loudly, irritated, my eyes closed. Then, sitting up quickly, "What is it? Travis? What's wrong?"

He puts his fingers to his lips, gestures for me to follow. I look at the clock: 3:07.

"What are you doing?" I change my voice to a whisper, remembering, suddenly, that someone else is in the house. "It's the middle of the night! Are you sick?" I reach out to feel his forehead.

He pulls away impatiently. "Come with me," he says urgently, and I follow him down the hall. Outside Lydia's shut door, he stops, waits. And then I hear it. Snoring. Loud snoring, cartoon variety. I look at Travis, cover my mouth as I start to laugh. But he is not amused. *"Mom,"* he whispers fiercely. "It isn't *funny!"*

He shakes his head, then goes back into his bedroom, slams the door. I go in after him, sit on his bed. "Travis . . ." He pulls the pillow over his head. I try to take it off and he pulls it more tightly over him.

"You can't breathe when you do that, you know."

"Who cares?" His voice is muffled, shaky with tears.

"Come out from under there. I want to talk to you."

"I don't want to talk. You're just *crazy*." He turns away from me.

I yank the pillow off, turn him over. "Now, you listen here. You listen to me. Don't you dare talk to me like that. I am your mother. And I am not crazy. I am . . . Things are changing, that's all, Travis. They are changing because they have to. And don't you slam doors at three in the morning, either! Some people are trying to sleep."

He watches me through narrowed eyes, says nothing.

Finally, I say, "Well, *what,* Travis? What's the big deal? So she snores."

"She woke me up! I have to go to school tomorrow! I have to get a good night's sleep!"

I refrain from commenting on this new interest in academic responsibilities, say instead, "Tomorrow's Sunday, Travis."

"Well, fine, but she probably snores every night."

"I suppose she might. But you'll get used to it. You really will. You'd be surprised what you can get used to. After a few nights, you won't even notice it."

"Who wants to get used to it? Who wants an old lady living here, anyway? She's not even my grandma."

"No, she's not."

"So why is she here?"

"I told you. Dad left. If we want to keep living here, we need a roommate to help pay for the mortgage. Remember, I told you that?"

Nothing.

"Travis?"

"Yes, I remember." His voice is quiet now, resigned. I hate that he knows what a mortgage is.

"What if she dies here or something?" he asks.

"Pardon?"

"What if she *dies* here?"

"Well, Travis, I'm sure that's not going to happen." My God. What if it does? I see myself on the phone, abstractly weeping, saying, "I don't know her medical history. She just moved in. But I think she's dead."

Nine

A LITTLE OVER A WEEK LATER, ON MONDAY MORNING, I sit alone at the kitchen table. Lydia got up early, had tea and toast with blackberry jam, and then went out with Thomas. She was going to accompany him to a doctor's appointment, and then they were going to an afternoon concert at Symphony Hall. Travis ate his Cheerios sullenly, then left for school without saying good-bye. Now I sit with a fourth cup of coffee, feeling my heart beat too fast and not caring. Maybe this is a good way to kill yourself: an exuberant overdose of caffeine, *I'm dying, I'm dying, I'm dying!!* could be my last thought. *Had to go!! Too painful!!*

Oh, what I want to do is hand my life over to someone else. That's all. And they could rearrange everything into something that would make sense. *There,* they could say; *now, was that so hard?* Well, for me, yes. It is too hard for me. I am no good at my own life.

I close my eyes, lean my head back, and begin to sob from a place deep in my stomach. I can't be alone. I don't want to be alone. I miss David so much, yes I do, I miss the presence of another person in my bed at night, even if he doesn't touch me; the reliability of someone else being there in the morning, even if they only shave and stare straight ahead into the mirror while you lean against the bathroom doorjamb with your cup of coffee, chatting hopefully. And I miss my son; I miss the way that he was before, when he trusted me, when he thought I could take care of him.

And then suddenly I stop crying, push wet strands of hair back from my face. What is the point in this?

First, I will go on a diet. This grief has put five pounds on me so far. I have to be careful. There are some women for whom sorrow attracts fat, and I am one of them. I will go on a diet and then I will take some adult education courses. Oh, but then I'll have to find some. And I'll have to go and register somewhere, fill in tiresome blank after blank, put an X in the "Ms." box. I've always put an X in the "Ms." box, but now it's pathetic. And I'll have to get dressed. I'm not dressed now; I don't get dressed right away anymore, Martha Stewart doesn't know what she's talking about.

I stare wearily at the kitchen table, at the swatch of sunlight that lies over the basket of paper napkins. The pattern on the napkins is illuminated; white-on-white roses. I never saw those roses before. I have lived my life blind.

I need to talk to someone. I go to the phone to call Rita, then stop. It's too early. Who, then? Louise and I have never been close. I haven't made any other real friends. There is no one. I have spent most of my life focusing on David, and he is gone. Nothing has rushed in to fill this void; there are no natural laws to make for an instant adjustment; humans are stupider than nature. I just have to go through this, that's all. By myself. It is all up to me, things are too much up to me and I don't like it. It is not exhilarating. It is not an opportunity to "grow." It is hard work; scary, lonely stuff; and I don't want it. I don't want it. I want my old life back.

I go to the phone, quickly dial David's office number. When his secretary puts me through, I realize I have no idea what to say.

". . . Sam?"

"How are you?" *I was just going to call you! Sam, I've made a terrible mistake.*

"I'm fine." His voice is wary. Wary! But we were married, we were married, for nearly twenty years!

I lean against the wall. "David." I squeeze the phone cord.

He waits.

"How come you did this?" I ask, finally.

"Sam—"

"I really feel terrible. And I don't know who to tell. I don't have anyone to tell who can understand what you . . . You were my *friend*. But you're not my friend. I don't understand how this happened, David. I don't get it, really; I literally don't. I mean, you didn't give me a chance. You never really told me what was wrong." Crying. Again.

"Where are you?" His voice is low. Impatient.

"I . . . In Paris, David. Where do you think I am? I'm home. Goddamnit, I hate you."

"Look, I'll come over after work. We'll talk."

"No! . . . Fine."

"I'll be there about seven."

I hang up, embarrassed for myself in front of myself. Oh, what do I want back? What? The bored tolerance of a man who finds not one thing about me charming?

The doorbell sounds, and I wipe my face, go to look out the peephole. It is King, the man who helped Lydia move in, holding the leashes of three dogs. No, four. Between the legs of the German shepherd is the ridiculous face of a Chihuahua, barking wildly at nothing. There are twin cocker spaniels on braided leashes, sitting patiently as bookends and looking up as though they are the ones that rang the bell.

I open the door and the dogs all rush forward. King pulls them back, smiles expectantly at me. "Hi. Want to go for a walk?"

"Well, I'm kind of . . . not dressed. I'm . . ." I see the same accepting kindness in his pleasant face that I saw before. "I've been crying," I say, laughing.

"Yes, I see that. Come for a walk with me. You won't cry anymore. Come on, go get your leash."

I start to say that I can't. But why can't I? I ask him to wait a moment, and go upstairs to dress. I select a blue sweater that is a flattering color for me.

When I walk down the steps with King, he offers me his arm, and I take it. Such a lovely thing. When did people stop doing it?

"Where are we going?" I ask. It's a perfect November day—just cold enough for a coat, the sun bright.

"Anywhere." He stops, holds out the tangle of leashes to me. "Dog?"

I smile, select the pink rhinestoned leash of the Chihuahua, whose hysteria has been silenced by the prospect of something interesting happening.

"DAD'S COMING FOR dinner tonight," I tell Travis. He is at the kitchen table, listlessly eating a snack of peanut-butter toast. He looks up at me, searching for a way to react.

"Okay?" I say.

"What for?"

"What do you mean, 'what for?' To eat."

He shrugs, pushes his plate away. "I'm done."

"What do you think we should have for dessert?" He'll help me, Travis loves to help make dessert.

"I don't care. What, is he moving back here?"

"Well." I put his plate in the sink, run water on it. "No. He's not moving back. He's just coming for dinner."

Travis nods, picks up his book bag, and starts out of the room.

"Where are you going?"

"Homework."

"Travis?"

He turns, annoyed.

"I think you should—you know, remember that this was not my idea. I mean Dad moving out and everything. None of it was my idea."

"I know."

"Well, you act . . . I don't know why you're so mad at *me*." But even as I say it, I realize I do know. He's mad at me for the same reason I'm mad at myself. Because although this was not my idea, it is my fault.

"I have to go do my homework."

"Fine."

I open the refrigerator, pull out the steak. I'm making beef Stroganoff, David's favorite. *God, that's good!* he said, last time I made it. *You can cook, honey; that you can do.* I slice the meat thinly, look out the window at the tree branches swaying in the wind. It's supposed to storm tonight. *A power outage, and David stays to take care of us, how could he leave?*

I rinse off the mushrooms, recall King pointing out a leaf on one of the trees we passed. "Maple," he said. "Their leaves look too big for the tree, don't you think? Like kittens' paws."

I'd asked him the names of the other trees we passed.

He knew them all, tried to show me how to identify a tree by looking at the bark, the leaves, the structure of the branches. I learned Dutch elms, oaks. Birches, of course. Black locust, whose blossoms he told me smelled like grape lollipops. "Cardinal," he said, about a sound we heard coming from the tops of one of the trees, "hear how it's like a whistle?" I asked if he could see the bird and he handed me the dogs' leashes and used his big hands to make a frame, and then I saw him, too. I learned blue jay (creaky gate) and catbird. "It *does* sound like a cat!" I said, and King smiled. "Ain't life a playground?"

"What are you doing with all these dogs, anyway?" I asked, when we stopped in a park to rest. And he told me walking dogs was his job for the day, he took jobs by the day. Just so happened that his assigned area was near my neighborhood. Yesterday he'd handed out samples of cheese at a supermarket. Smoked Gouda. Very good.

"I see," I said. I didn't really see. I think what he does is pretty nutty. But I like him. He's such a nice man, plain but really good, like bread and butter. And so easy to be with. Relief. I told him to come by tomorrow, if he could.

DAVID ATE LESS than half of what was on his plate. Clearing it, I ask, "No good?"

"No," he says, "it's fine. It's great. I'm just . . . I'm trying to cut down on that stuff a little. You know."

"Oh. Sure." He had half a glass of wine to my three, too. I put the plates in the dishwasher. I should have made chicken. Fish. No. I should have made something brand-new, oh God, of course I should have.

"Dessert?" I ask.

"Aw, Sam. I have to pass. But God knows Travis will

finish it." Travis had taken a huge piece of lemon meringue pie up to his room, then come down for another.

"Coffee?" My voice is thin, taut. "Want coffee at least?"

If he refuses that, I'll tell him to leave.

"Sure," he says. "But let me go and say good night to Travis. Then we can talk."

About what? I think. After Travis left the table, we went over money, what days were whose with our son. Then there was an awkward silence that lasted so long I had a strange impulse to burst out laughing. David was looking down and chewing at his lip, an old nervous habit, and it was no longer my job to remind him not to do it. He moved his spoon left, right. Left. I wanted to snatch it from his hand and say, "Look at me!" but I didn't know what I'd say after that.

"Be right back," he says.

I watch him walk toward the stairs. I have always loved how he looks from behind. The bit of hair over his collar. His broad shoulders, a good butt, even Rita always admitted that. I hear the stairs at the top of the landing creak in their familiar way. A father, going upstairs to say good night to his son. What has happened here? How have I lost this? I pour two mugs of coffee, bring them into the family room and set them on the coffee table. I sit at the end of the sofa, then move to the middle. I use my finger to quickly check the corners of my eyes for chunks of mascara, ruffle my hair to make it look fuller.

When he comes back downstairs, David says, "He's asleep already!"

"Yeah. He's been doing that."

He looks at his watch. "Eight-thirty?"

"He's been getting up earlier lately."

David takes his mug of coffee, sits at the edge of his recliner. He looks like he has a body-wide itch he can't scratch. He doesn't really want to talk, not about anything. He was just being polite, he feels sorry for me. "Where's your roommate?" he asks.

"Spending the night at her boyfriend's. Sometimes she does that."

"Really!"

"Yes."

"Well." David clears his throat, sets his coffee down *no good?* and then there is silence except for a slight humming sound from one of the lamps. *Quiet!* I want to tell it. *Can't you let me think? Can't you see I'm trying to do something here?*

"Sam . . ." David finally says, and as soon as he does, I am up and moving toward him. *Come back, come back, please come back,* is at the back of my throat.

I kneel at his feet, put my arms around his waist, hold my breath to keep from sobbing. I am horrified; somewhere over my head, a miniature version of myself looks down in disgust, hands on hips, head shaking. But there, there is the feel of his hand on the back of my head, his voice saying my name again, but softer. I close my eyes. And now his fingers are on my neck, so warm. I push my face harder into him. He cradles my head, wordless and still, and I open my eyes and see his belt buckle. Which I know. Here he is.

I close my eyes again, begin to kiss gently around the area of his zipper. The fabric smells warm, ironed, clean. I start to unzip his pants, hear him pull in his breath sharply. I stop, wait.

Nothing.

I finish unzipping, reach inside his underwear. *Let me.* I am aware of my own wetness, the sweet, specific ache of desire. *Oh, let me, let me.* He is flaccid. I rub, gently. Nothing. I pull my hair back, take him into my mouth. "Sam," he says. "Don't." But he does not push me away, and so I continue. In a minute, he will respond. And then I will say *I heard you, I heard everything you said at dinner but you don't mean it, you see? You can't mean it, we just need time, we just need to change a few things about the way we were together. You don't really want to leave, look how you still care for me.*

But he is still limp. What am I doing wrong? My knees hurt. I want to change position, but I'm afraid to move. I take in more of him, change my rhythm.

And now, still soft, David pulls away from me. I don't know where to look. Even in the worst of times, this has always worked.

I sit back on my heels, looking down at the floor, hear him zip up. My humiliation is huge in me, it holds me to the floor.

"I'm sorry," he says.

I nod.

"It probably isn't a good idea, anyway, Sam."

"No."

"I should go."

"Right."

"Are you okay?"

Nothing.

"Sam?"

"Yes. I'm . . . You should go."

"Is there anything else you needed to talk about?"

"No." Here, in my stomach, a blunt feeling of something landing. And then a slight nausea.

He stands, reaches down a hand to me.

"Just go," I tell him.

I hear the front door close, then his car door. I go to the

window, watch him drive away. I should have tried to re-call a scene from one of the adult movies we'd rented, something we tried a few times when our lovemaking had sputtered, then stalled. But when I think of those movies now, I can only remember how sorry I felt for the women—their terrible, flat eyes, their bad teeth.

The movies hadn't worked at the time, either. The last time we'd watched one, I, lying beside David in the obligatory flimsy black nightgown, aware of his erec-tion, had nonetheless asked, "Oh, God, what would their dads think?"

David had frowned, and I had stared at the screen, thinking, well, what *would* they think? Some of the girls had bruises—subtle bluish marks that the makeup couldn't quite cover. The background music was so ridiculous, and the moaning so loud and urgent it was completely uncon-vincing. "I think there ought to be some element of surprise in the plot," I said. "And there needs to be some vulnera-bility in the characters. In the men."

"What the hell do you think this is *for*, Sam?" David asked, then sighed and turned the TV off. Which I was glad about. Who could watch those things, really, and not laugh? Or weep? I always envisioned the girls coming home from those jobs, their heels *click clicking* back to too-warm apartment vestibules, to dented mailboxes with only bills in them, the girls' first names' indifferent initials.

He was trying to tell me something, renting those movies. Why didn't I listen? Once again, I feel a move-ment in my stomach, a nausea. I go upstairs quickly and vomit in the hall bathroom. After I flush and turn on the cold water to wash my face, I hear a knocking at the door. I open it to find Travis, his eyes squinting in the light. "Are you sick?"

I reach down to hug him, kiss his cheek. "No, I'm okay, honey. Go back to bed." I watch him start back toward his bedroom, then call, "Travis? Were you sleeping till now? Did you just wake up?"

"Yeah," he says sleepily.

"Okay. Good night."

What could I have been thinking? What if Travis had come downstairs? "What are you *doing*, Mom?" he would have asked. "*Gross!*" I would have pulled away quickly, fingered the button at the top of my silk blouse, blushing furiously, and David would have zipped up fast, covering his uncooperative penis that had lain in his lap like a grubworm. Actually, maybe it wouldn't have been so bad to be discovered. At least then David would have been embarrassed, too.

I gently close Travis's door and go into my bedroom, sit on the bed for a long moment. Then I remove my wedding rings and put them in my jewelry box. So many others have done this. I am not the only one. I am not the only one. But here, I am the only one.

I go down the hall and into Lydia's room, turn on her bedside light. It's a comforting space: a white afghan folded over a chair, a hardback book with a faded blue cover lying on the footstool, bookmark in place. A faint smell of lilac. I look around, feeling only a little guilty. There are photographs on the dresser, gold and silver frames on a white-lace runner. I pick up one of Thomas, hold it under the lamplight to see it better. He must have been a very handsome man, in his prime. His eyes are still an arresting blue, his gaze steady and direct. His ears are large and they stick out just a little; probably they used to embarrass him, but they seem distinguished to me, senatorlike. I also like Thomas's white mustache and the deep wrinkles in his forehead, reminding me of the beautiful lines you've seen from an airplane window, etched in the earth. It is such an intimate history I see here on Thomas's forehead. This is worth something, isn't it?

Maybe I should consider dating much older men. What's it like to love an eighty-year-old? When Thomas and Lydia go to bed together—and I know they do—what's it like? It must be so slow, it must be so exquisitely tender. I imagine a gentle old hand on my neck, sliding down my back, acknowledging each vertebra. I would not be bothered by any of his age spots; I would let in an older lover's touch like sunshine on a winter day, yes I would. And with an old lover, I could feel so young! *You're so beautiful,* he would say to me, oblivious of my recent need to hold small print away from myself. *My darling,* he would say. I pull Thomas's photo closer, close my eyes, open them to the blurry sight of his smile. I kiss it. Then I sigh, wipe my marks off the glass, put the picture carefully back on Lydia's dresser.

Oh, I envy Lydia her whole correct life: drinking tea out of her blue-and-white bone china cup every morning, dressed for the day in a wool skirt and white blouse, a pin with an elegant luster at her throat. She has a woman friend named Katherine who visits her regularly, who always wears a hat and gloves with her dark coat—button galoshes last time, too, defense against an early, thin layer of snow. She carries an old-fashioned purse and I love when she reaches in to get her hankie, or compact, or her candies in their flowered tin. I imagine a heavy fountain pen in that purse, the ink a peacock blue. I imagine an address book with gold-trimmed pages, each entry done in perfect Palmer script. A jeweled pillbox, a tortoiseshell comb. No Day-Timer. No Mace.

Katherine and Lydia have been friends for more than

sixty years, Lydia told me, exchanging recipes and child care and patterns for padded-shoulder suits in their early years; now going to museums and flower shows, to downtown department stores to share sandwiches for lunch, and to hospitals to visit friends—or, occasionally, each other.

Outside, I see a vein of lightning stab the sky, and then I hear the low rumble of thunder. A wonderful sound when you are in bed with someone you love. I watch the rain come down, hear how the sound changes from tapping to drumming. The urgency! It should be snow; but for this freakish run of warm weather, it would be snow. I wish it were. I wish the season would change definitively. I slip off my shoes and lie down on Lydia's bed, turn out the light, pull her beautiful rose-colored quilt over myself. I will sleep here, wrapped in the comfort of someone else's life, far away from those rings I left behind me.

I lie still, my hands folded across my stomach, listening to the anchoring sound of my own breathing. Sheets of water cascade down the window. Inside this house now suddenly too big, my boy and I lie down in our separate places and give ourselves over to the quiet repair of sleep. Outside, the sky weeps and weeps. Or so it seems to me. Times like this, everything in the world becomes personal.

Ten

IT TAKES ME A FEW DAYS TO TELL RITA WHAT HAPPENED. And when I do, she is her usual Sagittarius self. "I can't believe you made such a fool of yourself," she says.

"Oh, I shouldn't have told you. I knew I shouldn't tell you. I don't need recriminations now. I need support."

"I can't support you in something so stupid. What are you begging him for? Getting rid of him will be good for you!"

"Yeah, it's been great so far." I get out of bed, slide my feet into my slippers. "I have to go. I have to get dressed."

"It's noon there!"

"I'm well aware of that."

"I thought you were getting dressed first thing, these days."

"That didn't last. Martha Stewart is crazy."

"Well, we all know that. I don't know why you would ever take a suggestion from her in the first place. Everything she tells people is just a set-up for failure. She's a misanthrope."

I open my closet, look for something to wear. "I don't think Martha's so bad. I think I want her for a friend instead of you. When I look at her magazine, I feel soothed. When I talk to you, I feel like hanging myself."

"All right, listen. Listen to me. I would not be your friend if I didn't say this to you: I don't feel sorry for a victim who keeps choosing to be a victim. That's what you're doing. You're not even trying. You're just sinking deeper and deeper into feeling sorry for yourself."

"No, I'm *not*!" Yes, I am.

"Have you looked for a job yet?"

"No." Yes. I asked at the nursing home and they said they didn't need anyone. Then I looked in the paper and everything was too hard.

"Well, get a job!"

"What can I do? Who's going to hire a forty-two-year-old woman whose only job experience is singing in a band?"

"A lot of people would."

"I have to go. I'm late for a lunch."

"You are?"

"Don't get excited. It's with my mother."

"Oh, great, that'll help you right out."

"Well, Louise called. She told me Mom sounded like a wreck when she talked to her last week. She wants me to check up on her—I've been kind of ignoring her."

"Why doesn't Louise check up on her?"

"Let's see now. Could it be that I live in Massachusetts and Louise lives in Montana?"

"Well, don't stay there long. She'll make you crazier."

"I suppose."

"Call me later tonight."

"What for?"

"Just do."

"You call me. I don't want to spend the money."

"David is still supporting you."

"I know, but I don't want to take any more money from him than I have to."

"Well, there you are! That's the kind of thinking you need to be doing!"

I hang up, go into the bathroom to wash my face. I feel like I just got a fake *A*. I'm not interested in saving David money. I'm interested in being mean to Rita.

"HONEY," MY MOTHER says sadly, "look at you."

We are sitting at my mother's kitchen table, chicken salad sandwiches before us that have been cut into fours and anchored together with confetti-topped toothpicks. She is objecting to my unwashed hair and my outfit: a pajama top over gray sweatpants. She herself is wearing a sheer white blouse tucked into black-and-white checked pants, and a red cardigan sweater. Earrings that are cherries.

"I'll change before Travis gets home; don't worry about it. I just worked out."

She doesn't bother to call me a liar. I bite into my sandwich, pull a grape out of my mouth, and fling it onto the plate.

"What are you doing?" she asks, frowning.

"I don't like grapes in chicken salad."

"Well. It happens to be good."

"You know, all through school, you put butter on my meat sandwiches. And I told you I didn't like butter on my meat sandwiches. But you did it anyway. I didn't *like* butter on meat sandwiches, and I don't like grapes in my chicken salad!"

"Well, I'll tell you what. You just call up *Good Housekeeping* and you tell them that they don't know what they're doing. I'll bet they'd appreciate that. They'd probably give you a free subscription."

"They probably would."

Silence.

Then I say, "Listen, how are you, Ma? Louise is worried about you."

"Me?"

"Yes."

"Well, I have no idea why. You're the one she should be worried about!"

"She said she thought you were depressed."

"She should know better than that. I don't get depressed. I'm absolutely fine."

I sit back in my chair. "Oh, why not? Why don't you get depressed?"

She stares at me, wide-eyed.

"Why *don't* you? I mean, everybody does, once in a while. Everybody *should*, once in a while. It can be good for you to feel bad."

She takes a bite of her sandwich. "This is *delicious*."

"You know? Seriously, Ma."

She puts down her sandwich, looks at me. "You want to know why I don't get depressed? I'll tell you why. I never saw the point of it, Sam. I don't delve into things too deeply. It's better that way."

"How would you know? You don't have any means of comparison. You glide along like . . . You never even . . . When did you ever let anyone get close to you? I mean really close, to the real you."

She looks at me, a long-lasting thing that makes me feel as though I'm being slowly drunk. Finally, "I don't know how you can say that, Sam," she says quietly.

"Well, it's true! You have this . . . It's *impenetrable*, your constant, crazy cheerfulness. It's an insult! It *keeps* people from you."

She nods, slowly. Then there is the ridiculous sound of the kitchen cuckoo clock, signaling the half hour. I look at my watch. "I have to go. Oh, Ma, I'm sorry. I'm sorry

I said that. I'm just . . . I don't know, I guess I needed to yell at someone. I'm sorry." I stand, reach for my coat.

She takes our plates to the sink, starts running water.

"I'm really sorry. I'm a jerk."

"It's all right. You've got a lot on your mind. I know you're not yourself."

I stand watching her. I don't know what to do. I've got to go.

"I'll see you later."

"Sam?" She shuts off the water, turns to face me. "You'll find this out when Travis gets older. But your children never really grow up for you."

I start to say something, then stop.

"You protect your children. You must always protect them."

"From what, Ma?"

"From everything that's sad, or wrong, or scary. I mean, you try. That's what you're supposed to do."

"But . . . That's not what I believe. I believe children are entitled to the truth."

"How much truth, Sam?"

I don't answer. What is the answer?

"I know I embarrass you, I've always known that. But I have to get through life in my own way. It pleases me to be happy. And it pleases plenty of other people, too. Yes, it does. Louise, for example."

"Are you serious?"

"Louise does not have a problem with me. She loves me very much. She may not tell you that, but she does." I stare at my mother's carefully made-up face, and suddenly I see that same face many years ago, shortly after my father died, when she came out of the bathroom after having been in there for a very long time. "Now!" she said. I was sitting in the hall, spinning jacks, and I looked up at her. "I think this style is much better, don't you?" She showed me some modification she'd made to her hairdo, and I nodded, then returned to my jacks.

What occurs to me, now, is that what my mother had been doing all that time was weeping. With astonishing quiet. And that when she was done, she'd washed her face, fixed her hair, put on lipstick, and then gone out to the kitchen. She turned the radio on low and made dinner so that it would be ready when it always was. And then she smiled and chatted empty-headedly or fussed at her daughters all during dinner, preempting any kind of real conversation, preempting any questions, and then she put her daughters to bed, still smiling, still dispensing random advice about this and that, and her daughters squirmed and rolled their eyes and felt their love lessen year by year, eroded by embarrassment, by a terrible, defeating kind of resignation that told them she would never be different. But what did Veronica do after she put us to bed? I wonder now. And I imagine a mother who took a mask off her face, then pushed hard into a pillow to weep for the loss of her husband, for the loss of the life she was supposed to have, for the only man she ever—I actually gasp, thinking this now—loved. And it comes all at once to me, it comes at this instant, that my mother simply lost too much and repaired herself in the only way she was able; that, in fact, she is continuing to repair herself, hour by hour, the pendulum of the cuckoo clock swinging in the light and the dark of all the days that have passed since my father died at this same brown wooden kitchen table.

"Ma," I say. "I'm so sorry."

"For what, honey?" There it is, the vacant brightness in her eyes, evidence of the invisible amputation that I have missed forever, until now. She comes over and hugs me. "Don't be sorry. I'm just fine. You tell Louise that, all right?"

"Yes," I say. "I'll tell her." And then, "Want to come to dinner tomorrow night?"

"Not tomorrow. I've got a date with a new fellow." She makes a giddap sound. "A Charlton Heston look-alike and I'm not kidding. It's his son that I want you to meet, by the way."

"Okay."

She blinks. "Really?"

"Yeah."

"Well, I . . . He *is* divorced, honey, a couple of times. Well, three. But he doesn't have any children. And he—"

"It's all right. I'll meet him."

I slide my coat on. My arms feel unreal to me, sewn on. At the door, my mother says, "His name is Jonathan. J-O-N-athan, that kind. I'll have him call you."

"Okay."

"Don't rush anything, now. This is just for fun."

"Ma . . ." My mother waits, expectantly. One eye-brow has been drawn in slightly lower than the other, and it is nearly more than I can bear. "I won't rush," I say. "Don't worry."

As I am stepping into the car, my mother leans out the door to call, "How about if I come for dinner Thursday night?"

"Fine," I call back, realizing I forgot I asked her.

Eleven

I AM STANDING AT THE LIVING-ROOM WINDOW, WATCH-ing for King's car. He is taking me to the employment agency he works for. "You don't need any experience for lots of these jobs," he'd said. "Alive and ambulatory, you're in their *A*-plus bracket."

Lydia, who is on the sofa with a large-print novel, sighs and puts her book down.

"What," I say.

"Are you grinding your teeth? Is that the noise I'm hearing?"

"I'm not grinding my teeth."

"I could have sworn."

"Well, I'm not."

"Are you nervous?"

"No!" I cross my arms tightly over my chest.

"It's hard, I know. But you'll be all right."

I go to sit beside her. "It's just, I've never felt so . . . I mean, I think about getting a job at McDonald's, and I worry that I won't be able to work the cash register."

"Oh, I think you could probably manage that."

I check my watch, get up to look out the window again.

"He's not due quite yet," Lydia says. "Don't worry. He won't be late. He's not the type."

"What do you mean?"

"I mean he cares. He pays attention. He's not the type to disappoint."

"Right. As opposed to the type I married."

Lydia hesitates, then says, "I wonder if I might ask you something."

I turn to face her. "Of course."

"Did you think life would be easy all the time?"

"No!"

"Are you sure?"

A horn honks, and I jump up. "Here he is! I'll see you later."

"Good luck. And take your time, I'll be here when Travis gets home. I'll have him help me make dinner— he's quite good at making meatballs."

"Thank you. And Lydia?"

"Yes?"

"I really didn't think it would be easy all the time. I just didn't know how weak I was."

"Well. That's where you're wrong." She pulls her cardigan up higher over her shoulders, resettles her glasses on her nose. "You'll see."

KING WAITS FOR me while I fill out the application and have an interview. Then he takes me to a diner. He orders coffee; I order the cheeseburger platter deluxe.

"So?" he says.

"So, it was easy!" I shed my coat, toss it into the corner of the booth. I feel good. I feel great.

"I told you."

"The woman who interviewed me looked like she was twelve."

"Ah. The senior staff member, then."

"They said they'd call as soon as *tomorrow*."

"They could."

"Maybe we'll get a job doing something together!"

"I'm moving mattresses tomorrow. Warehouse."

"Oh. Never mind."

My burger is delivered, and I take a bite, then say around it, "I told my mother I'd go out with someone she knows."

"Oh, yeah?"

"Yeah. I wanted to do something for her."

"What about you? Is it something you want to do?"

I salt my french fries, eat one. Two. "Not really."

"You might have a good time."

I shrug, offer a fry to him, which he refuses. I wonder if he's dieting. If he lost weight, he'd be a very attractive man. But I would miss something. I've grown accustomed to his size. It's comforting to me.

"Your husband was an asshole," King says suddenly.

I look up, stop chewing.

"I'm sorry. I shouldn't have said that."

"It's okay. It's true."

"It's hard to hear criticism about someone you love, though. I know that."

I start to say I never really loved David, then don't.

IN THE CAR on the way home, I tell King, "I feel so comfortable with you."

"Yes."

"I mean, from the very beginning, I felt as though we were friends." I shiver a little. The car is cold.

He turns up the heat, reaches behind him for a blanket, tosses it on my lap. "Me, too." And then, "You know, I've just started to date out of the personals. So don't feel bad about your mother fixing you up."

"Really? Have you had good experiences?"

"Mostly, I'm too fat." It is mild, without rancor, the way he says it. "I tell them on the phone that I'm heavy, they usually say it's no problem, but then I show up and most of the time they get that look. You know? That look?"

"So what do you do?"

He shrugs. "I tell them never mind. I say it's okay. I go home and read, or go to the movie by myself."

"Well, they're . . . They ought to give you a chance."

"Yeah," King says, smiling, and suddenly I see him as a little boy, home from school, innocent and hungry, holding pulpy papers in his hand that he will offer up to his mother. And then he is himself again, pulling into my driveway. "Here you are."

"Thank you," I say.

"Thank *you*."

I laugh. "For what?"

"I don't know."

I open the car door, and he says, "Well, I *do* know." I wait, expectantly, and he says, "I'll tell you another time."

Twelve

EARLY SATURDAY MORNING, LYDIA AND I ARE SITTING AT the breakfast table looking through the personals ads. We're seeing if anyone looks better than the blind date I have set up with Jonathan for tonight. "Here's one," Lydia says, squinting at the tiny print. "He's forty-three, he's financially secure, he likes dining out, travel, and walks along the beach."

"Oh, they all say that. Honest to God. Read a few more. They will all say that. What I want to know is, when I go to the beach how come I don't see hundreds of available men walking up and down looking for women? You know, expensive sweaters wrapped around their shoulders, airline tickets in their pockets?"

"Well, of course it *is* almost winter."

"I know, but even in summer I never see any."

Lydia considers this, frowning, fingering the handle on her teacup. "I'll bet there were some available men there. You probably just weren't really looking."

"No," I say. "They weren't there. There were just families yelling at their kids not to drown and teenagers walking around like billboards, acting as if their bodies would never change. They're so oblivious to the fact that they'll get older. Sometimes I want to grab them and say, 'Hey! I used to look just like you! Ha-ha-HA!!' "

"Yes," Lydia says. "That's what I want to say to you sometimes." She sips her tea.

My God. Of course that must be true. Of course it must! What's a little cellulite next to a face full of deep wrinkles? What's a face full of deep wrinkles next to infirmity? When does the time come when you stand in front of your grown-up woman's mirror and feel contentment for what you see? Ever?

"Well now, look at *this*," Lydia says, pointing to the ads. "This really does sound good—he's an artist—a painter; he has season tickets to the ballet; he likes big dogs. Oh, but he's a much older gentleman. He's more for me."

"You don't need anyone," I say ruefully. Lydia is wearing a gift from Thomas: an ultra-soft, navy blue robe with a thin line of red trim. In the pocket of the robe had been a folded-up sonnet about sleep, one of Thomas's favorites that he had copied out for Lydia in his tall, back-slanted script.

"I know," Lydia says, smiling. "In fact . . ."

"What?"

"Well, maybe I shouldn't say this yet. I'm not absolutely certain, after all. But Thomas and I are thinking about getting married."

I sit back in my chair, wordless. I see Lydia at the altar, her veil being lifted. And there is Thomas, his face illuminated with love and hope, bending down to kiss her.

"What do you think?" Lydia asks.

"Well, I . . ." *What about me???* "I think it's wonderful, Lydia. I just . . . That's really wonderful! When?"

"Well, at first we thought June, of course. But then, considering our ages, Thomas thought maybe we'd better just go ahead and do it as soon as possible." She looks meaningfully over the top of her glasses at me.

"So. You'll be moving out, then."

"Yes, I'll be moving into his place."

Damn. I'll have to find another roommate. I recall seeing a sign only yesterday on the bulletin board at a bookstore: FEMALE COLLEGE STUDENT SEEKS ROOM. CAN TEACH JAPANESE. At the time, I'd thought idly of calling her, thinking it would be nice to have one more roommate; the heating bill has been much higher than I thought it would be. Now I think I'd better go to the bookstore as soon as it opens this morning and get the number, have the woman over for an interview right away. It might be nice, having a young Japanese woman around. That black hair, that soft voice. I am making terrible assumptions, I know, I am possibly even being racist, but I can't help it. The woman will sit at the kitchen table in a beautiful turquoise kimono, cut an orange into six even slices.

And then I look over at Lydia and my fantasy dissolves into regret. I have loved sharing a house with her. I like it when she sits at the kitchen table slowly folding towels while I make dinner. I like seeing the strip of light coming from under her door when I go to bed at night; it makes me, however irrationally, feel safe. We occasionally watch old black-and-white movies together late at night, sighing with equal implausibility over young Robert Mitchum, over Clark Gable. We have begun to talk like girlfriends, to reveal the small and intimate things that one collects like cards for a good hand on the way to forging a real friendship. I know that Lydia likes pea soup with the ham bone in, gin rummy, the jolting thrill of cold sheets at night, a certain brand of outrageously expensive cold cream that comes in a frosted glass jar with a pink top. She will wear only silk slips. In some ways, in such a short length of time, Lydia has become a better friend to me than Rita. But now she is going to leave. I try smiling, but I feel terrible. Abandoned again. Perhaps this will be a condition, like anemia: Chronic Abandonment.

"It won't be for a while, Sam. I want to give you at least a month's notice. And as I said, I'm really not completely sure, yet."

"Well, why wouldn't you do it?" I ask. The phone rings, and I ignore it.

"Why wouldn't I? Oh, I don't know. I kind of like my independence. And to tell you the truth, I've really enjoyed living here with you. I feel as though I've gotten younger, in a way. And I adore Travis—we've become real pals."

"I know," I say. Travis has been teaching Lydia to play his latest computer game. Last night, jealous, I stood in the hallway with the laundry basket on my hip, peeking into Travis's bedroom. I saw Lydia sitting beside Travis, listening to him tell her things he had never told me. The only thing he has told me recently is that Lydia's bird recognizes him, calls him by name whenever he speaks to it, whereas every time I say anything to it, the bird falls silent. I can't imagine a parakeet saying, "Travis," but never mind.

I go over to the sink, rinse out my cup. "I do wonder," Lydia says, "if getting married at my age isn't awfully foolish."

"I don't think so," I say. "And I hope if you have a wedding, I'll be invited."

"Oh, of course. You and Travis. And that King fellow, I'd like him to come, too. Very pleasant man. And a wonderful cook."

True. On a few occasions now, King has made dinner for all of us. He never measured anything, always succeeded in making something we all, even Travis, liked.

Last time, King presented us with chicken roasted with some exotic herbal combination, tiny new potatoes, green beans, and a chocolate mousse pie we had all marveled at.

"You could make this," King told me that night, watching me eat a huge second piece. "I'll teach you." He tells me that all the time, that I can do things. Sometimes I want to say, "It's all right. You don't have to say that. I'm not so sad today." But I never do. Instead, I save his confidence in me as though his words were silver dollars, knotted in a silk scarf and kept hidden in a dresser drawer.

Travis comes into the kitchen, still sleepy-looking at ten-thirty, and heads for the cereal cabinet. "Can Mike Oberlin come over today?" He squats down to reach for Cheerios, his back to me. He needs a haircut; his pajamas are wrinkled; between the bottoms and top I can see his winter-white skin. He reminds me at this moment of a bird newly hatched from the shell. Were he younger, I would pull him onto my lap and hug him, bury my nose in his neck to breathe in the rich scent of child-sleep. Instead, I set out the milk for him, get him a bowl and a spoon, tell him of course Mike can come over. I relish these small returns to normality. I'll be wonderful to Mike. "Wow, your mom's cool," Mike will say, lying on Travis's bed with his shoes on, about which I will say nothing, not one word. "Yeah, I guess," Travis will answer, full of pride.

Travis fixes his cereal, then heads for the family room and the television. He'll turn on MTV, I know, and I feel the usual stab of regret that he's not watching *Sky King* or *Fury* instead of women's breasts shoved into leather brassieres, ravaged-looking young men howling out sociopathic lyrics while they walk around sets that look like Armageddon. I've decided to let Travis watch occasionally instead of making it more alluring by disallowing it. Anyway, as he has repeatedly pointed out, everyone else watches it. He *has* to. When he told me that, I imagined him sitting in the lunchroom at school with other boys who were discussing the latest videos. "You see Madonna air-humping?" I imagined one boy saying, and Travis answering, "Yeah!" and giving the thumbs-up sign. This depressed me, so I revised the scene to have Travis respond by saying, "Air-humping? What's that?" and then finishing the lunch I made him, all of it.

Lydia folds the personals, drinks the last of her tea. "I'd better get moving. Katherine and I are going over to the mall to do a little shopping." She goes to the sink to wash her cup, dries it, and puts it back in the cupboard. I put my mug in the dishwasher, then go to pick up the message on the machine. It is Jonathan, confirming our date for the evening, telling me that the restaurant he decided on is pretty fancy, just so I know what to wear. I hate this.

I call King, leave him a message telling him what time to come over. He's going to baby-sit for Travis—Lydia won't be home and David is out of town on business. Probably not alone.

"Dad has a girlfriend," Travis told me, last time he came back from spending the weekend with David.

"Really?" I asked, and Travis nodded.

"Did you meet her?"

"Yeah. That's how I know."

"What's she like?"

He shrugged. "I don't know."

"Well, what does she *look* like?" I asked, to which Travis again replied, "I don't know," in an irritatingly dreamy voice that made me feel like shaking him.

"Does she have blond hair?"

He thought for a moment, then said, "Red. It's long."

"Uh-huh," I said. "Well, that's all right. It's all right, don't you think? For him to have a girlfriend?"

Travis didn't answer. And I didn't ask any more questions.

Thirteen

At five in the afternoon, I head for Travis's room to tell him it's time for Mike's mother to come, they'd better wait downstairs, she'd called saying she was in a hurry. Outside the door, I hear the sound of muffled giggling. I smile, wait. I want to eavesdrop a little. Sometimes I write down the good stuff in a journal I've been keeping since Travis was born.

Apparently they are on the phone with someone. "Tell her you'll meet her at the movie," Travis says, and I hear Mike say, "Okay, so why don't I meet you right outside the movie. Seven o'clock tonight." He hangs up and the boys begin giggling louder.

Oh, what is this? I think. *They're too young for dating!* Then I hear Travis say, "How long do you think she'll wait?"

"Probably about five hundred hours," Mike says. They laugh again, louder, little hyenas; and I understand that Mike has no intention of going, that whoever the girl is will be standing there, holding her plastic purse and not looking around anymore after a while, just standing there. I push the door open, announce brusquely to Mike that his mother is coming, he should get downstairs and wait for her. Then, pointing to a Baggie full of chocolate-chip cookies, "Are those the cookies I made?"

"Yeah." His collar is turned up in the back and I want to stomp forward and turn it down. Hard.

"Give them back to me," I say.

"*Mom!*" Travis yells.

"Sorry. I need them."

Mike hands me the bag. He looks quickly at Travis, then away. He will tell his mother on me, no doubt. "You know Mrs. Morrow?" he'll say, "the one whose husband dumped her? She's nuts now." Well, the hell with him. The hell with his mother.

Later, I will make Travis call that little girl back and set her straight. Then I'll tell him that he'd better learn some things about how to treat girls, starting right now. I can't wait to give him this lecture. If he interrupts me, I will take away MTV from him for one hundred years. And what a pleasant century it will be.

"WHOA! YOU LOOK *great*," King says, when I open the door.

"Well," I say. "Thank you." I am wearing a cobalt blue dress, belted tightly at the waist. It's short, shows off my legs, and the color has always been good for me. I do look nice, even if the weight I've gained recently is making the belt feel like a pretty instrument of torture. I have makeup on for the first time in weeks, and I've fancied up my hair with hot rollers. Joy is at each of my pulse points.

King, dressed in a gray sweat outfit, is carrying two videos. "*Terminator One* and *Two*," he says, "do you mind?"

"I don't care what he watches. I'm mad at him."

"How come?"

"Oh . . . long story," I say, and look away. Because the truth is, I realize now, I overreacted. I don't know all the circumstances. Maybe the boys had some legitimate complaint against this girl. Maybe she had done something really terrible to them. But if so, they could have handled it another way. It's David I was punishing, not them.

"Where are you going tonight?" King asks.

"Oh, out to dinner, some fancy place. I don't want to go. I'm a nervous wreck. This feels so silly. *Dating.* What a dumb word!"

"You'll relax after you meet him. It's hard, this part, the part right before they ring the bell. Doesn't feel great to be on the other side of the door either, take it from me. Why don't you come and sit down with me."

I follow him into the kitchen, sit at the table opposite him. It feels so strange, sitting in this homiest of places wearing heels and sheer-to-the-waist panty hose, and a dress I have to be careful not to spill on. I hope there's nothing smeared on the seat of the chair, making a mark to which my date will point later, saying, "There's, uh . . . I believe there's something on your dress."

The kitchen light is such a nice yellow when it's dark out like this. It's so cozy. Why can't I just stay home, change into my own sweatpants, and watch movies with the boys, make some popcorn drenched with butter, loaded with salt? Why do I have to walk around outside in high heels, feeling the bitter November wind at my ankles as though it is sniffing them, asking *Are you crazy? Why don't you have socks on?* It's supposed to flurry tonight, maybe it could get bad. I'd better stay home.

"I'll bet I know what you're thinking," King says.

"What?"

"You're thinking of what you could possibly do to stay home."

"I am not."

"Listen, forget about it. Stop thinking about what might happen. Just sit here and let's talk. About anything."

"Okay." I fold my hands before me, try to think of something to say. My mind is absolutely blank. I am an imbecile. When my date tries to make conversation with me, I will only smile vacantly, like a Kewpie doll with feathers sticking out of her brain.

Finally, King says, "So. Got any job prospects for Monday?"

"Oh! I'm glad you said that, I meant to tell you. They did call me. I can have my choice—Laundromat attendant or receptionist. For a whole week!"

"Take the Laundromat thing."

"You're kidding."

"No."

"But isn't that kind of . . . humiliating?"

He smiles. "Why?"

"I don't know. Have you done it?"

"No, but I would. I like those kinds of jobs."

I nod, then say gently, "Didn't you ever think maybe you'd like to go to college, you know, get a good education, some great job?"

"I went to college."

"Oh, I'm sorry. I just assumed . . ."

"It's okay."

"Where did you go?" I ask casually. I'll need to be careful, tell him without seeming insincere that it doesn't make any difference, really, where you go to school.

"MIT," he says, and then, "do you have any popcorn?"

I point to the cupboard over the refrigerator. "MIT?"

"Yeah."

"The Massachusetts Institute of Technology?"

"Yeah." He pulls down a package of popcorn, brings it over to the microwave.

"What did you study?"

"Astrophysics."

"And did you finish?"

"Sure."

"So . . . why do you walk dogs?"

He turns around to look at me. "I like it."

Travis comes into the kitchen, sits down at the kitchen table. "Hi, King," he says pleasantly. This is so when he's nasty to me it will have a better effect.

"Hi, Travis," King says. "Want some popcorn?"

"Sure!" He stares sullenly at me. I stare back, then make a face at him. I'm good at this. I used to sit at the kitchen table with Louise, fighting silently behind our mother's back. Oh, the venomous stares we mastered, the contemptuous fury we could communicate in a split second's time.

The doorbell sounds and I start so hugely my hands fly apart.

"*Mom!*" Travis says.

I am going to throw up, right now.

"I'll get it," Travis says. And then, from the hallway, he yells, "Mom! It's that guy for you. He has *flowers*!"

Oh God, I think.

I look helplessly at King.

"Well," he says, "where do you keep the vases?"

Fourteen

WHEN JONATHAN AND I ENTER THE RESTAURANT, I HEAR a piano playing softly. In the far corner, I see a smallish black man, dressed in a tuxedo and a crooked black bow tie, seated behind a baby grand. He is older, his hair gray, his face lined. He is smiling—sadly, I believe—and playing elegant background music. He sees me staring and nods at me. "I know," I feel like telling him. "I don't want to be here either. Let's go somewhere I can wear jeans and you can play what you want."

"Two, for eight o'clock," Jonathan tells the maître d', who looks as though he has been stuffed into his suit. Were he not so smug-looking, I would feel sorry for him. "Certainly, Mr. Schaefer," the man says, checking a name off in a cream-colored register. "Right this way."

Oh, fine. *Mr. Schaefer*. Jonathan's been here a hundred times. No wonder he's perfectly relaxed. I never saw the point in going out to fancy restaurants. It's not that I don't appreciate good food; I love good food. But why go to all this trouble? Why put on fancy clothes to eat?

I follow the maître d' to the table, Jonathan close behind me. I don't like having him so close behind me. Probably hairpins are sticking out of my French twist. I could have runs in the back of my nylons; I forgot to check. I have never learned to walk quite right in heels; I always wobble. I have never liked dressing up for any reason and I will never, ever do this again. It's my life.

Plus I hate Jonathan. Who can't even be honest enough to spell his name with an *H*. Stupid prep school name. The name of a man who walks around flinging his hair back off his forehead, talking endlessly about sailing.

When my chair is pulled out for me with a flourish, I sit down, furious. What is the point of all this formality? Why should my chair be pulled out for me? Do I look incapable of pulling a chair out for myself? Why doesn't the maître d' pull the chair out for *Jon*athan? Why must it always be the women doing these circus tricks? And then, watching the maître d' pull the chair out for Jonathan, I think, *Oh. Never mind.*

Well, here we are. Only a couple more hours to go. I smile tightly at Jonathan, then at the white-coated waiter, who has glided smoothly as a swan to my side. I know his type. He will pour coffee starting low and then let his arm rise up spectacularly high, as though the stream should be roughly comparable to Niagara Falls. And he will sneak up on us, using ridiculous silver tongs to place sculpted pieces of butter on our bread plates. And everything he does will be done with an air of distant disapproval.

"Good evening," he says, and I jump.

"Oh!—Good evening," I say, and wish so much that I were at home, asleep.

"Would you care for a cocktail?" the waiter asks.

Would I care for a cocktail? I would care for about ninety cocktails. "Yes, a glass of white wine, please," I say. I hate white wine. I like red wine. Out of jelly glasses, like the gangsters in movies. But I think it might be wrong, red wine. Lightning-fast, the waiter recites a list of choices for white wine. Show-off. "I'll have the first one," I say. "The first one you said."

The waiter nods, turns to Jonathan. "A gin martini," Jonathan says. "Bombay Sapphire. Extra dry, extra cold. Two olives. Straight up."

"Very good, sir."

"Excuse me," I say, and when the waiter turns to me, I tell him, "I'd like to change my order to what he's having."

"Certainly."

"Sorry."

"It's quite all right." He glides away.

I smile at Jonathan. "So!" I clear my throat, look down at my purse. What's in here? A lipstick, some tissues. A few bucks.

"Are you nervous?" Jonathan asks.

I look up quickly, laugh, and then, to my absolute horror, snort.

Tomorrow I will kill my mother.

"Me, too," Jonathan says.

"Pardon?"

"I'm nervous, too."

"No, you're not."

He smiles. "I assure you, I am. I'm just sneaky about it."

"So do you . . . what makes you think *I'm* nervous? Is that why you asked that question? Because you think I am? Nervous?"

"It'll get better in a few minutes," Jonathan says. "Honest."

"Right." I lean forward a little, try to relax my hands, which have been clutching each other, rigor-mortis style.

He is handsome, there's no doubt about that. I wish I could freeze time so that I could stare at him for as long as I want. Thus far, I have taken polite little looks. He is blond, his hair nicely streaked; his eyes a deep blue. He wears a pair of tortoiseshell glasses that I like very much. He is tall, slim. What the hell is the matter with him that he has to have blind dates?

Our drinks are delivered and we both take a sip. I lean back in my chair.

"See?" Jonathan says. "It's better already, isn't it?"

"Yes. It is." Inside my pointy shoes, my toes uncurl.

IT IS OVER dessert that Jonathan brings up Veronica. "According to my father, she's quite an extraordinary woman."

"Oh, *yes,*" I say. "She really is." I take another bite of crème brûlée. It is delicious. It is so delicious! It makes me happy, the rough burnt-sugar surface, the smooth insides. Maybe I'll have another one. If I can have two martinis, I can have two desserts. The silver spoon I'm using is so elegant, so *right.* Look at these thick linen tablecloths, these lovely ivory-colored candles with their gentle, flickering flames, their flattering glow. I should go back to Tiffany's and get some candleholders. I was right, when David first left, to want to live this way. This is the way to live.

I take another bite, rub my tongue against the roof of my mouth. It feels wonderful. I look at Jonathan's mouth. Sexy. Deep inside me, a pleasant stirring. I want to kiss him. Oh, I want to kiss him. Later, I will kiss him.

Or now.

I stand up, go over to his side of the table. "I just want to do something," I say. I bend down and kiss him lightly on the mouth. Then I go back to my side of the table.

"There," I say.

"Well, thank you," he says. "That was nice." And then, "Are you . . . all right?"

"I'm *fine*." I sigh, rest my head in my hand. I wonder where my shoes are. Well, they couldn't have gone too far.

"I'm afraid we've had a bit too much to drink," he says, but his voice is kind, and rich, and he makes our overindulgence sound stylish.

"Yes," I say. "We certainly have."

"I don't usually—"

"Oh, me either!" What friends we are, able so soon to complete each other's sentences!

"You know, Jonathan," I say, "you are a very good-looking man. *And:* I would like to kiss you again."

"Well," he says. "Likewise."

"Should we do it here? Or should we go and make out in the car with the heater turned up?" I am quite pleased with my forwardness. This is really very good for me. I need to do more of this, yes, I do.

"Why don't I get the check," he says.

Oh, he's paying. What a wonderful, wonderful man. So . . . Gregory Peckish. I feel for my shoes, slide into them, and then stand, only a bit unsteadily. "I'll just go to the bathroom," I tell him.

I should have said "powder room." That would evoke the image of me sitting before a beautiful gold mirror, a vase of fresh flowers nearby, freshening my makeup, rather than sitting on a toilet. "Just want to powder my nose," I add, lightly touching his shoulder as I pass by him. There. All fixed. See? Life is easy. Full of choices and quick remedies, if only you look. There's no reason in the world to mourn one relationship when another is so easy to find. Why, Jonathan is reading the same book as I am!

After I use the toilet, I stand before the mirror, put on

lipstick, then blot it. I arrange my hair with my fingers, pull down on a strand to make it rest near one eye. I put on a little more eyeliner. Then a touch more blush.

I have always been a champion kisser, and I have a feeling Jonathan is, too. I can't wait to get back to him. I am a woman in my forties, and I know what's up. I can do whatever I want. I take in a deep breath, straighten my belt, head back to the table. This urge is growing stronger and stronger. Well, good. It's good. I'd thought I was broken. I'm not broken. I am an attractive woman, out with my new friend Jonathan, who is a very attractive man. My mother is quite good at this fixing-up business, I will thank her; yes, I will send her a pretty little bouquet and on the card will be *"Thanks."*

No. More.

On the card will be, *"You were absolutely right."*

No. Not that much.

Well, *something* will be on the card to tell my mother what a good matchmaker she turned out to be. Maybe I'll call Stuart Gardner, that guy who called before, the other one my mother recommended. Maybe I'll just be a dating fool, have a stable of studs. A blond, a brunet, and a redhead. None of them with male-pattern baldness. None of them on Viagra.

When I arrive back at the table, Jonathan looks up at me. "Ready?"

"Oh, yes," I say. "Yup."

OF COURSE WE do not make out in the car. We make out in his bed. I am in my forties and so is he, and we have admitted to each other that we have in our lifetimes had our share of back trouble. And so here I am lying on the bottom, and here he is lying on the top, and he is kissing me and I could not be more content. On the weekends when David has Travis, I will live here, and Jonathan will bring me champagne when I lounge in the tub after we make love. He will bring me champagne with a strawberry floating in it, and he will read to me from a book of poetry by Pablo Neruda.

He unzips my dress and I panic for a moment, wondering about the state of my bra; then remember that it's a push-up, a nice one, and I am eager for him to see it. It's got lots of lace.

I feel him pulling my dress down slightly. Then he stops, kisses my neck to make for a pleasingly painful pause. The man is a master. I should pay him.

He pulls my dress down farther, kisses my collarbones, moves down, stops just above my breasts. I pull lightly on his hair, inadvertently moan. He pulls my dress down to my waist and kisses my breasts through my bra. And now, finally, there are his smart fingers undoing my bra and his mouth at last on my bare skin. He runs his hand up my thigh, and I think I might burst with lust. And then, somehow, my bra is over my face, the underwire poking into my right eye.

"Hold on," I say, laughing, and start to pull away.

"Oh, no," he groans. *"Don't."*

"No, I just want to . . . wait a second." What I'll do is just take everything off. Well, maybe not everything. No. Everything.

But he is squeezing me tightly, holding me down, kissing me harder than before. It is not entirely unpleasant. But then, suddenly, it is.

"Jonathan," I say. *"Wait a minute!"*

He pulls back, his eyes narrowed. "What the fuck is this? You want it just as much as I do."

I breathe out an astonished laugh, feel myself descend with a lurch into instant sobriety. "I just . . ."

"Forget it. The hell with it." He sits up at the edge of the bed, turns on the light. I regret that his clothes are still on, while I am in a state of undress that is sexy no more. No, not anymore. I pull down my bra, fasten it, sit up, and pull my dress onto my shoulders. With some difficulty, I zip it.

Jonathan takes one sharp look at me, then looks away. He pulls a pack of cigarettes out of the bedside-stand drawer, lights one.

"You *smoke*?" I say, and the whole, whole card house falls down, down, down.

OUTSIDE, I LOOK up at the night sky, blink back tears. It's too cold to cry. It's clear, the moon full, the stars like pinholes in black velvet. On the lawns I walk past are the reaching patterns of moon shadows, cast by the bare limbs of trees. I walk carefully, slipping often. "Goddamn men," I say, out loud. "They're all pigs. All of them."

But Travis. He won't be a pig. I'll make sure of it. I may not ever contribute much to this world, but the one thing I will do is make sure Travis is a gentleman. A gentle man. I am going to start paying very, very close attention to him, and shape him so that he will come out like a gay man, but be straight. Unless of course he wants to be gay. But it doesn't look good for that. Signs of inattentiveness and carelessness abound.

I slip again, and this time fall gracelessly onto my side. My purse slides a few feet ahead of me, then stops as though it is looking back, playing a game. I start to get up, but then instead turn onto my back. It's not so bad, here on the sidewalk. It's restful. I move my arms and legs, checking for pain. Nothing terribly wrong—nothing broken, anyway. The door to a nearby house opens. I see a yellow rectangle of light, then the silhouette of a woman in a bathrobe leaning out. "Hello?" she calls. "Are you all right? Miss?"

I struggle to my feet. "I'm fine," I say. *Liar.* "I just fell."

"I *saw.* My *goodness*!"

"Well, it's slippery, you know! You'd fall too, if you were out here wearing three-inch heels!"

The woman closes the door.

Oh, I hadn't meant to sound so defensive. I should have been nicer, asked the woman to use her phone to call a cab. I brush snow off my coat—funny, I'm not so cold now—and continue walking.

A car slows down, and I quicken my step. It is Jonathan, come to beg forgiveness. Well, he is not forgiven. Then the car pulls over, and I see that it is not Jonathan, it is a bunch of teenage boys. The window rolls down and the boy riding shotgun leans out, starts to say something. Then, seeing me more clearly, he says nothing, rolls the window back up, and the car drives away.

Pigs.

When I finally arrive home, I let myself in the back door, go into the kitchen, and upend the vase of roses Jonathan brought me into the garbage. Red for romance. Right.

"Hello?" King calls. He comes into the kitchen and leans against the doorjamb, watching me. I rinse the vase out, shove it back into the cupboard.

"Didn't go so well, huh?"

"Ha!" I fling wet hair off my face, kick off my heels.

"What happened?"

"Well. For one thing, I ended up walking home."

"Really!"

"Yes, that's right. I walked home. And let me tell you, that was the best part of the evening."

"You walked all the way home from the restaurant?"

I look up from unbuttoning my coat. "Yes! Well . . . No. It was . . . from his apartment, all right? It was from there. But it was still far!"

"What happened, Sam?"

I burst into tears. And when King comes toward me, I hold up my stained evening bag to keep him away. "No," I say. "Don't." I weep silently for a moment, then stop suddenly and say, "I am sorry to tell you this, King, because you're a man. But men are assholes. Every single one of you. This can never change."

"Well. Not every one of us."

"Yes, you are. I'm sorry. But, yes, you are."

"You must be freezing. Go change out of those clothes. Then come down here and I'll make you some tea."

"I don't want any tea. And I don't believe I want to talk. Thank you for baby-sitting. I mean, I'm grateful. I am. But I do not want to talk to you."

He shrugs. "Okay." He starts for the closet and his coat.

I regret myself instantly; King has never been anything but kind to me; none of this is his fault. "Wait," I say. "I'm sorry. Don't leave. I'll go change."

In my bedroom, I throw my dress on the floor, then kick it into the corner. I pull out a pair of jeans and a faded blue sweatshirt from my dresser drawer, start to put them on, then throw them on the floor as well. From another drawer, I pull out plaid flannel pajama bottoms and a long-sleeved T-shirt. I change into them, add thick socks and my old, battered terry-cloth robe. In the bathroom, I take off my makeup and contacts, and put my glasses on.

On my way back downstairs, I peek into Travis's bedroom, then tiptoe in to watch him sleep. I want to kiss his forehead; and I want to wake him up and say fiercely between my teeth, "Listen, buster, don't you *ever* treat a woman the way I was treated tonight!" I do neither; instead, I stand beside him, cotton-headed, realizing the alcohol hasn't quite worn off yet.

In the family room, a grainy black-and-white movie is on TV. A dinosaur is shaking a skyscraper around in his mouth, his eyes rolling unconvincingly from side to side. People cling to the side of the building like ticks. When King sees me, he turns off the television, folds his hands over his stomach. Waits.

"I think this was date rape," I say, finally. "Almost."

He starts to say something, then stops.

"I mean it!"

"I'm sorry."

"Well, what did I expect? This is what always happens, one way or another."

"Come on, Sam. It's not what always happens. You know that."

I stand still for a moment, wondering if I have enough energy for a good debate. He reaches forward, pulls my glasses off my face, and polishes them with his sweatshirt. "You can't even see," he tells me.

"Can too." I watch as he rubs the glasses, holds them up to the light, rubs them again, and then places them carefully back on. The gesture is so tender it makes me start crying again, for all that is not tender in the world.

"Was Travis good?" I ask, finally, through my tears.

"Yeah," King says gently. "Travis was fine." And then, "You know, I've never been too good at fighting, but I could go over there and sit on the guy for you. Where's he live?"

"That would be great," I say, laughing, imagining the scene. The elegant Jonathan would be flattened cartoon-like beneath King.

Then I stop laughing, feel the tail end of my drunkenness wash over me like a mild flu. I realize I am not particularly capable of anything. "King?" I say. "Could you just stay here for a while, just until . . ."

"Yeah, sure."

"Okay. Good."

The phone rings. "Who's calling so *late*?" I say, and then, of course, know. "It's him, the bastard." I glare at the phone.

King picks it up, says hello. Then, "Yes, she's here." He looks over at me. "Do you want to—"

"No!"

"She'd rather not," King says. Then, turning slightly away from me, "Probably you shouldn't call her any-more. That'd be my advice." A pause, and then, "A friend. I'm her friend."

I feel a rush of feeling start in my center and then spread until I can feel it in my fingertips, in my toes. Safety, is what it is. And the blanketlike relief of it is awesome.

"YOU *WALKED* HOME?" Rita asks, later that night.

"Well, it wasn't that far. A couple of miles." Now that I have the outraged sympathy I was looking for, I can feign nonchalance.

"It's *winter*! You were wearing *heels*!"

"It's not winter yet. It's still November."

"It's always winter in Massachusetts. Except when it's August and then it's hell."

"I didn't have a choice. I had to get out of there fast."

"Was he really that bad?" Rita asks. "Maybe he was just frustrated. Maybe he thought you were teasing him."

"No, he was that bad. It wasn't just nasty. It was scary."

"Well, don't go out with *him* anymore."

I hold the phone away from myself, look at it. *Don't go out with him anymore.* Great advice. Gee, and I was going to call him tomorrow, ask him to come over and maybe hold a knife to my throat.

"I'll talk to you tomorrow, Rita. I'm going to sleep."

"Wait, listen, I was thinking about coming out there. How would that be?"

"It would be *great*, what do you think? I'd love to have you come out here! When?"

"Next week, I thought. Right after Thanksgiving. I'll come on Saturday, leave the next Saturday."

"A week?"

"Yeah. Why, do you think that's too long?"

"No! Well . . . yes. But no."

"Don't worry. I'll be helpful. I'll fold all the socks. I'll chop the onions for dinner. I'll help you find a new roommate."

"Ugh. Don't remind me."

"Maybe you'll get someone better."

"Nobody would be better than Lydia. You'll see."

After I hang up the phone, I stare at the ceiling, thinking. Rita hasn't visited for a long time. Last time she was here, Travis didn't have any front teeth. Now he doesn't have a father, and his mother dates sociopaths.

And yet.

I turn off the bedside lamp, realize that nothing hurts. I take in a deep breath, as though the inhaled air will check around and let me know if that's really true. It is.

Fifteen

"Mostly, you only make a change," the balding Chinese man tells me. I stare at him for a moment, uncomprehending, wondering if perhaps he is offering advice, then realize he is talking about money: I am to *make change*.

It is nine o'clock Monday morning, and Mr. Lee is orienting me to my job at the Laundromat, leading me down a long aisle of square white washers. Gigantic dryers line one wall, round glass openings like portholes. A solitary figure, a thin, older man, stands folding at a waist-high table. His movements are slow and deliberate, graceful. He is matching exactly the corners of the thin, striped towels he pulls from the metal laundry basket.

"And also you make sure"—Mr. Lee turns to me, shaking his finger in my face—"no one steal! They try steal carts, dials from washer, who knows? Steal anything you not watch!" He resumes walking again, and I meekly follow. He is wearing neatly pressed tan pants that end just above the heels of his Nike sneakers, and a light blue shirt with the sleeves rolled back. He has gray metal bifocals and a hearing aid that occasionally emits a high, squealing sound which Mr. Lee angrily adjusts—stopping in his tracks, grimacing, looking upward, and muttering.

"Also you clean up little bit," he says. He smiles at me, revealing small, tea-colored teeth. His voice is softer now, kind. "People throw trash, forget. You keep nice, people want come in, do wash! Okay? Okay?"

"Yes," I say. "That's fine."

"You bring laundry?" the man asks.

"Pardon?"

"You bring laundry?"

"Did *I* bring laundry?"

"Yeah-yeah!"

"No, I . . . I have a machine at home."

He turns away, heads for the little office in the back of the room. "Too bad. Fringe benefit. Do laundry."

"Oh. Well, that's nice. Maybe tomorrow."

I follow him into the office, hang my jacket on the coat tree after Mr. Lee removes his. He points to an old wooden desk. "You sit here. Shut door." Pointing next to a small, square hole in the wall that is located above the desk, he says, "All business through window. Not let customers in office! Business only through window. Professional! You keep door locked." He hands me a set of keys. "You go home, you give keys afternoon person, come at two."

For a moment, I am frightened, wondering why Mr. Lee is so adamant about keeping the door locked. Is there that much money in the office? Are there robbery attempts here? I'm glad I'm on the early shift. Probably most criminals like to sleep late.

He opens a desk drawer, shows me a bag of Hershey's Kisses. "You like candy, huh?"

"Well . . . yes. Sure."

"Aha! I think so, first time I see you. Detective! Candy fringe benefit."

Next he shows me large plastic containers of quarters

and dimes, a tray for paper money. "For make change!" he says, and then, narrowing his eyes suspiciously, "You know how?"

"To make change?" I ask. "Yes."

He smiles widely, a flash of gold. "Some people, don't know how. Dumb."

"I see."

"Okay!" he says, zipping up his jacket. "Other Laundromats now. I got more, go check." He opens his wallet, hands a small white card to me. "You have question, you call. You get my wife, she tell you what."

"Yes, all right. So, just to . . . let me just make sure, here. I make change, and clean up, is that right? And then at two o'clock the afternoon person will come. He *will* come, won't he? I have to be home for my son when he gets back from school."

"He come, he come!" Mr. Lee says impatiently. "Steven. He come, all the time. Never miss!"

"Okay," I say. "Just checking."

He is almost out the door when he turns back to yell at me, "No dye! No one using dye!"

"Right," I say. "The signs say so."

"Not enough!" he says. "You watch!"

"I will."

He gets into an older model white Cadillac. He can hardly see over the top of the steering wheel, yet the car suits him. I sit down at the desk, open the newspaper, pour a cup of coffee from the thermos I've brought. I hear a sound and, looking up, see the older man who had been folding laundry standing in the window before me. "Change for a dollar?" he asks. He has a thick Southern accent.

"Quarters or dimes?" I ask, thinking, *Professional!*

"Both," the man says, and I pour a shiny pile of coins

from my hand into his. The simple exchange fills me with pleasure. "Thank you," he says, and then, "You new?"

"Yes. Yes I am. I'll be here all week."

"Okay," the man says. "Don't worry. I'll help you." He leans in closer, clears his throat. "My name is Branch Willis, and I know everything about this place. I been coming here for years."

"I'm Sam."

"Uh-huh." A moment, and then, "You *are* a woman, right?"

"Right. It's Samantha."

"Well, I'm sorry. I'm sorry. You *look* like a woman, don't get me wrong! It's just you never know. These days, especially. I didn't mean to offend you."

"I'm not offended."

He starts to shuffle away, then turns back to say, "You mostly stay in there, in the office, like he said. But you can come out, too. Up to you. You're the boss."

"Okay," I say. "Thank you." I sit back down at the desk, smooth the dollar bill Branch gave me, put it in the drawer. The door opens and another customer comes in, a woman with a little girl.

"Here's Mary!" Branch yells over to me. "And her little girl, that's Lisa. How y'all doing?"

I stand, stick my head out the window, smile. The little girl must be around four years old, a solemn and beautiful face, two tight blond braids. She clutches a baby doll tightly to her chest, carries over her shoulder a tiny diaper bag.

Minutes later, the door opens again, and an extremely tall and handsome young black man comes in wearing sunglasses, carrying a denim laundry bag and a blaring boom box. He looks around, selects a washer, then sets the boom box carefully down on the floor beside it. He turns the volume up louder.

Lisa covers her ears and turns to her mother, who turns away. Branch is minding his own business.

"Excuse me," I shout. Then, louder, *"Excuse me!"*

The man turns to look at me, raises his sunglasses. "What." Even from this distance, I can see that his eyes are bloodshot.

"Could you . . . just . . . turn that down? Please?"

"Fuck you." He dumps his laundry out. Black jockey shorts fall to the side of the tall heap, a floral print pillowcase. My God. Everyone does laundry.

I sit back down, move my chair out of sight of the window. Make change and clean up. That was the job description. Not suicide. I stifle an impulse to take one more peek at the man's dirty laundry, then pop a Hershey's Kiss in my mouth and suck nervously. I pull the phone closer to me. 911, that's the number. Isn't it? *Is* it? Of course that's it. 411 is information; 911 is emergency. "Yes, I wonder if you could help me," I imagine saying. "I'm in a Laundromat and one of my customers is murdering everybody."

But then when I chance another look out the window, I see the man sitting in a chair next to Lisa, helping her change her baby doll's diaper. "Say what?" he says to her. And then, smiling brilliantly, "Yeah, she's a *good* baby."

I ARRIVE HOME a full forty-five minutes before Travis is due. The phone rings as soon as I hang my coat up. "I'm returning your call?" a young woman's soft voice says. "About the room? I'm the one who put the sign up?"

"Oh!" *The Japanese girl. The one who will so beauti-fully peel oranges.*

"Yes," I say. "Thanks for calling back. I wonder if we could get together. To . . . you know, talk about this."

"When?"

"Well, I guess . . . as soon as possible."

"I'm not doing anything now. If that's all right. I could meet you now. Where do you live?"

I tell her the address and the girl says, "That's close. I can be there in five minutes."

I go into the kitchen to set out two mugs. Herbal tea, we'll have. And then, spying the bowl full of fruit I keep on the table, I push it closer to the mugs. Just in case.

When the doorbell rings, I open it to find a girl as Asian-looking as Gidget with a buzz cut.

"GUESS WHAT?" I tell Travis. "I found us a new room-mate. She'll move in December first."

"Oh, man," he says wearily.

"She's very nice. You'll like her."

"Well, who *is* it?"

"She's a student, honey. She can speak Japanese! Her name is . . . well, she changed it. It used to be Elaine. But now it's Lavender Blue."

Travis's eyes widen. "Lavender *Blue*?"

I shrug.

"I don't know where you get your ideas, Mom."

"I called her references, Travis. She's very quiet. Keeps to herself—she'll be no trouble. She used to live on a farm in Indiana and now she's a student at Boston University."

"She's going to live in the basement?"

"Yes."

"Doesn't she care?"

"Why? It's nice in the basement. It's not like a *basement* basement. There's carpeting. She has her own bathroom. And there's room for everything she needs."

"She must be weird to want to live in the basement."

"She's a student, honey. You don't mind living in those kinds of places when you're a student."

"Huh. *I'm* not going to when I'm a student."

"Well, maybe not. But she is. And I hope you'll give her a chance. Look how much you like Lydia."

"Fine, but her name isn't Lavender *Blue*."

"I'm sure you can just call her . . . Lavender."

He shakes his head and sighs, but then, with a look of pleasant expectation, heads for the refrigerator.

The phone rings and I answer it, watching Travis pull the lid off a plastic container. Cold spaghetti. His favorite.

"So! How you like?" the voice asks.

"Mr. Lee!" And then, since I have been warned by the employment agency not to have customers call me directly, "How did you get my number?"

"Phone book! Only three 'Morrow'! You number three! How you like job?"

"Well, it was . . . fine. It was just fine."

"You like, I give you full-time. Just between you, me."

"Oh, well, thank you. But I think I'll just do the week. I can't really commit, you know. To full-time."

"Oh," he says, disappointed. And then, "Okay! But you come whole week, then! Every day!"

"Yes, I will."

"Who was that?" Travis asks, when I hang up.

"Mr. Lee. The boss from where I worked today. He wanted to hire me full-time."

"Wow," Travis says, with an honest admiration that

makes me want to weep. "The boss called you the first day?"

"That's right."

"That's good, isn't it?"

"Sure," I say. "It is."

Sixteen

❖

LATE IN THE AFTERNOON ON THE DAY BEFORE THANKS-
giving, I pull up in front of David's building. I had a little
trouble finding it, despite David's clear directions. In the
end, it was Travis who told me where to make the last
turn. The tree-lined street is short and narrow, rather
artistic-looking, I think jealously. There are stately black
lamps, old gas types that have been converted to electric,
and now, as I look at them, light up as though showing
off. I cut the engine, turn to Travis. "You ready?"

"Yeah, I guess."

"I'm sure you'll have a very nice time."

He shrugs.

We open our car doors simultaneously, and I follow
Travis up the walk, watch as he rings the doorbell. I
wonder when this will be normal, this sharing of a boy,
these deliveries of him back and forth as though he is a
package to be signed for. I reach out to smooth his hair
back, and he lets me. He is feeling bad, too, then, despite
his attempts at indifference. "You don't have to stay," I
say suddenly. "We can just visit, and then I can bring you
home."

"No, it's okay. I want to see Dad." The buzzer sounds,
and he pulls the heavy door open.

It's an interesting building: old, but extremely well

maintained. A lot of mellow oak in the entryway; pretty leaded glass windows, mosaic tile, a nice wooden elevator. We ride to David's floor without speaking. Travis's foot is tapping rapidly; my heart feels as though it is going at about the same rate.

When David opens the door, I nod rapidly, as though he has just said something I couldn't agree with more. "Here he is," I say, but Travis is gone, well into the apartment that he already knows.

"Come in." David clears his throat, stands aside. He is wearing his dark blue V-neck sweater, my favorite, and a crisp cologne, also my favorite. For a moment I wonder if this is for me, then remember that of course it's not.

I drop Travis's duffel bag at my feet. "He's all set for four days," I say, and then hear a mournful reverberation in my brain. Four days! Four days! What will I do by myself? Lydia and Thomas are gone, off visiting Thomas's niece for a week. King will surely spend Thanksgiving with his parents. I will be completely alone for the first time since . . . And then I remember: Rita will be here Saturday. That's right, I'll only have two days alone and then Rita will come.

"Come see my room," Travis yells from somewhere down the hall, and I turn to David, asking permission, I suppose.

He nods, gestures for me to go ahead.

I pass through the living room, look quickly around. Good-looking furniture, a white (!) sofa, some new artwork on the walls. I always wanted a white sofa and he always said no. Why does he have one now? What is the change that allowed for it? It's a nice one, too, plump and inviting. Needs a throw, though. Or some pillows, some color of some kind. Against one wall is a stereo system that looks to me like Darth Vader, and over the windows are tiny blinds, which I have always hated. There. I feel better.

Travis's room is small, but quite nice, really. There are bunk beds covered with bright red spreads. In the corner is a yellow beanbag chair, a black lamp beside it. A number of airplanes hang suspended in the air. Dental floss, I see, when I get closer. Oh. Clever. A small television and a portable computer sit on the desk in the corner, and a telephone, too, the transparent variety that Travis always used to ask for. Yes, it's a very nice room. The curtains are better than those he has at home, the carpet, too. All right, and the furniture, too. But Travis's favorite teddy bear is at my house.

Travis jumps up when I come into his room. "See?" he says, pointing. "I have a bunk bed here."

"That's great." Am I getting a cold? I feel like I'm getting a cold.

"Want to sit on it?"

"Well, of course."

"Top or bottom?"

"I don't know. What do you recommend?"

"Top, definitely, top. Sit up there."

I climb the ladder, crawl out onto the bed, sit at the edge. I see David from the corner of my eye, standing just outside the room. Why does he do that? Why doesn't he come in here? Must he so continually tell me he's no longer a part of us?

I look down at Travis, at his excited face. "It's so *high*," I tell him.

"*Right!*"

"Is this the standard height?" I ask David.

"Don't worry. He won't fall out."

"I wasn't worried about that," I say, though the truth

is I was envisioning Travis lying still on the carpet below, his neck at a terrible odd angle.

"Come have some coffee with me," David says, and Travis and I both hear the real message.

"I'll just . . . be in here," Travis says, turning on his television.

In the kitchen, David pulls a chair out for me, then sits down himself. "*Do* you want some coffee?"

"No," I say. "Thanks." I cross my legs, widen my eyes, force a smile. "So!"

He smiles back, a little embarrassed, and I want to touch his wrist, to reassure him. I still feel something for him. I still want to take care of him; it is a reflex.

We sit quietly for a moment. A car starts outside, drives away.

"I'm fine," I say, finally, "if that's what you want to know. I'm doing just fine. Really."

He nods. "Good. And you're sure you have enough money?"

"Yes, David. We worked it all out, remember?"

"Well, Travis said you were going to get another roommate."

"That's right. Lydia is moving out."

"Ah. Well. That didn't last long."

"It wasn't because she didn't like living there," I say, too quickly.

"I know," he says, also too quickly.

Silence again. The phone rings, and David makes no move to answer it. And I cannot answer it, and this realization picks up my insides and drops them back down. Divorce is a series of internal earthquakes, that's what it is, one after the other.

"You know, David, this is so . . ."

"I know."

"Well. The main thing is, do you think Travis is all right?"

"Yes. Do you?"

"I guess. Although . . ."

"What?"

"I don't know. Nothing. I mean, I don't know what I'm supposed to tell you anymore, David. Do we talk about all the little things? Or just . . . you know, major things."

"What do you mean by 'major things'? Did something happen?"

"No. Not really." I had thought to tell him about Travis and his friend calling that little girl. But why?

The phone rings again.

"Your phone," I say.

"Yes, I hear it. They'll leave a message."

They'll. Why doesn't he just say "she"?

I shift in my chair. Something hurts in my back. I'm getting pneumonia, maybe that's it.

"Travis said you had a date," David says, looking past me, out the window.

"Yes. And Travis said *you* have a girlfriend."

Now he looks at me, contrite. "Yes. I've wanted to tell you. But I didn't know what to say, really."

And my *skin* feels warm to me. My hands, holding each other, they feel warm. I must be getting a fever. One hundred and one, one hundred and two. Three. "You know, I don't feel too well, David. I think I'd better be getting home."

"You're sick?"

What phony concern. I nearly laugh out loud. I want to tell him not to bother. I want to slap his face. I want him to embrace me and beg forgiveness and come home with me and *stop* this! Doesn't he understand that if he doesn't stop this it will be too late?

Oh, but it is too late. It is too late.

I stand up. "I don't know if I'm sick. But what if I was? You have Travis, so I wouldn't have to worry about him. We're all set. I'll take care of myself. I'm fine. I really am." I zip up my jacket, manage a smile, though all I can see is the girlfriend's silk robe, hanging on the back of David's bathroom door. I'm sure it's there. I'm sure it's silk. I'm sure it smells like perfume. And like David.

"Well. You have a nice apartment, here."

"It's . . . you know. For now. It is nice. Thank you."

I go into Travis's room to say good-bye. He is lying on the top bunk, listening to his Walkman. "What's wrong?" he asks, when he sees me. He takes off his headphones.

"Nothing! I just wanted to say good-bye."

"Were you crying?"

"No! I'm just tired, you know? I'm going to go home and take a long soak in the tub and then read a big fat book and eat a big fat candy bar. I'm actually pretty excited."

"What kind of candy bar?"

"I thought I'd stop at CVS and scope it out."

"Yeah. They have a good selection."

"I think I'll get the killer-size Snickers."

"Boring."

"Well." I kiss his forehead. "*I* like them. And if I were eating one right now, *you* would want a bite."

"I know. But they're still boring."

"I'll see you. Eat a lot of turkey. Put gravy all over everything, even the cranberry sauce."

"I will. Mom? Are you making pumpkin pie?"

"Well, of course I'm making pumpkin pie. I'll save some for you."

"Okay. Shut my door on your way out?"

I shut his door, head slowly down the hallway. Travis has never had a Thanksgiving without me. But he seems all right. He does. He seems all right. I don't know whether to be relieved or depressed.

David accompanies me to the front door. "Take care of yourself," he says.

"I will." No one else to do it. I start to open the door, then turn back suddenly. "You know what, David? I still don't know what you wanted. I just don't know what you *wanted*."

"I . . . We're just different," he says softly.

I swallow hugely.

"Look, I want you to know that I don't think there's anything wrong with *you*, Sam. But the way we lived together, it wasn't what I wanted. Sometimes I feel like there's this fire in my belly that I need to feed all the time. And it wasn't being fed."

Fire in his belly? Fire in his *belly?* That needs to be *fed?* Oh, I can't *wait* to tell Rita that he actually said such a thing. This is great. A white couch, and a sudden transformation into Robert Bly. This must be his girlfriend's influence. Probably they're taking a New Age communication class together, holding hands every night and checking in with each other before they fly off to the land of dreams, which they record in their journals and share with each other over breakfast.

As though sensing my thoughts, David shifts his shoulders, his old, familiar sign of discomfort. "That sounded stupid, I know. But I don't know how else to say it. What I mean is I feel like I was always . . . *yearning,* whereas you were so happy with everything the way it was. And it started making me crazy. I don't accuse you, Sam. I don't fault you. We just never really connected. I mean, *you* don't think we did, do you?"

"No!"

He smiles. "Well. So."

"Tell Travis to call anytime he wants to. Happy Thanksgiving."

"Same," he says, and closes the door softly after me.

I walk down the hall, smell something with curry cooking. (A neighbor, sticking her head out of her door and into the hall, a wave of blond hair over one eye: *Oh, David! Hello! I thought I heard you out there! Want to share a little something with me tonight? Again?*) I push the button for the elevator, wait a second, then head quickly for the stairs. It is too big, what I'm feeling. I have to keep moving. I still . . . what is it? Love him? *Is* that it? Need him? Want him?

I miss him; I love how he looks, how he dresses, how he smells.

I get into the car, look into the rearview mirror and see, for one split second, Veronica. This is all her fault. At the heart of things, I am my mother's daughter, always making too much out of too little, really *liking* the scent of country-fresh furniture polish and the sight of a clean bathroom. I am a prisoner of genes wearing aprons.

But it *was* enough for me, the way our family lived. Maybe that was wrong; maybe I should have wanted more. But I didn't. I knew things were far from perfect, but I was content sitting outside with my coffee on spring mornings, admiring the daffodils Travis and I planted, thinking about what to make for dinner that night. I liked attending school conferences with David and listening to dressed-up teachers talk about our son. I liked going to the hardware store every Saturday, all of us in jeans and T-shirts; and I liked watching videos every

Sunday night while we ate takeout Chinese from the cartons. I would actually wake up on Sunday mornings a little excited about doing it, even though we did it every week. Perhaps because we did it every week. It was *enough*, to light a fire in the winter so that we could all toast marshmallows, to look out the window in the summer at David mowing the lawn and Travis riding his bike around in self-absorbed circles, a half-moon of dirt above each elbow. When I got up in the morning and set the table for breakfast and smelled the first whiff of French roast and unrolled the newspaper to lay it flat on the kitchen table by David's place (the comics by Travis's), that was *enough* for me. What is the matter with me, that this was enough?

I shiver, put my hand to my forehead. Where is the fever? Where is that damn fever? I need it. I need it *bad*, as Travis would say.

He is still my son. No matter where he is, he is still mine.

Seventeen

AT TWO O'CLOCK ON THANKSGIVING DAY, I AM LOOKING at a fashion magazine I brought home from the drugstore. I also got eleven other magazines, three tabloids, a Snickers bar, a box of chocolate-covered cherries, four colors of eye shadow, three lipsticks, bubble bath, a party-size bag of Chee-tos, floral-scented furniture wax, and a designer razor—very nice, made to fit precisely into the hand. Well, into the designer's hand. I lick my fingers and turn the magazine pages by the lower right-hand corner, slowly. Louise used to read magazines like that, me sitting beside her on the sofa. It seemed a queenly ritual. I had always wanted to turn the pages, too, but Louise wouldn't let me. Well, look how far I've come. My very own stack of magazines. They have helped me not to think about Travis eating dinner with David and his girl-friend. A little.

Most of the clothes in the magazine look like a kind of joke to me. And if the style isn't, the price is. But here is a perfume sample—free. I tear it out, rub it on my wrist, inhale deeply. Not bad. I'll buy some, if ever in my life there comes a time to wear perfume again.

A twenty-one-pound turkey is in the oven. Janis Joplin's "Ball and Chain" is on the stereo. I have always loved this song. When I was in the band, the guys and I used to gather in the basement bedroom of the keyboard player, where our equipment was kept; and we would play albums through the band's huge speakers. Not just Janis; we played Monk, and Vivaldi, Hank Williams and Keith Jarrett. We played Earl "Fatha" Hines and Dinah Washington. James Brown, Howlin' Wolf. Sometimes I would look around the room, at the way the guys' appreciation looked less like joy than anguish. Every nuance in the music was played out in their faces—you could see it in the movement of their eyebrows, the shape of their mouths, the rhythm of their nodding. Fingers tapped on knees, feet were often going, too. Their eyes were closed; I would have said they were not exactly on the planet Earth. One night after a gig when we were eating cheeseburgers at an all-night diner, the guys all agreed that they'd rather be blind than deaf. I said no; if it came to that, I'd want to see. But often, when I was onstage and deep into a song, I could feel it, too, that singular lift, that sense of being filled up and taken over. Complete, and wanting nothing else.

I was good; I was a very good singer. I was once approached by a man from a well-known talent agency who wanted to back me as a solo act. He told me he'd bankroll everything, down to my wardrobe. "I'd need to bring the band," I said, and the man said no, I didn't need them. I said I wouldn't be interested, then. "Are you *crazy*?" the man said. "I'll get you a record contract! You get out on the road for me for six months and I *guarantee* I'll get you a hell of a contract." I still remember every detail of this—the guy leaning forward in the red leather booth of the club where we were playing that night, his cigarette burning low. He pushed his Scotch off angrily to the side, yanked up his sweater sleeves. He was wearing an expensive gold watch. He was a handsome man, balding, but handsome. "I don't think so," I said, and the man said I'd better be sure, he wouldn't ask again. "I'm sure," I said, and the guy sat back, blinked. "I don't get it," he said. "Do you have any idea what you're turning down, here?" I stared at my hands, shrugged. "What," he said, "are you sleeping with one of them?" I looked up quickly, denied it. But I was. I was sleeping with the lead guitarist—Stevie, we called him. And I wouldn't leave him. Later, when I told him what I'd turned down, he told me I was crazy. Which hurt my feelings. "I didn't want to do it without you," I said, and Stevie said, "Sam, I'd have taken a deal like that in a second." Of course he would have. He was already interested in someone else, though I didn't know it until a few weeks later.

No offers like that had ever come again. I sang until I got engaged to David; and then I stopped singing.

I pick up the CD cover, look into Janis's eyes. She was a musical genius who never did find love. Never did. Janis had a beauty that men probably never appreciated. It was in how she felt things, not how she looked. Although there was a kind of hard beauty to the way she looked, too. It was there. But men came, and then just left her. All the time. At least she had something to do with her anguish—nobody sings pain like she does.

I look at my watch. Time to baste the turkey again. I love basting the turkey. Every time I open the oven, I eat some stuffing. Early this morning, just as the sun was starting to come up, I made stuffing the old-fashioned way, dipping slices of stale white bread into hot water, tearing it apart, seasoning it with fragrant leaves of sage, and onions sautéed in an ocean of butter. I made cranberry sauce, and when it was done put it into a dark blue bowl for the beautiful contrast. I was thinking, doing

this, about the old ways of gratitude: Indians thanking
the deer they'd slain, grace before supper, kneeling before bed. I was thinking that gratitude is too much absent
in our lives now, and we need it back, even if it only takes
the form of acknowledging the blue of a bowl against the
red of cranberries.

I'm having baked sweet potatoes, and white mashed
potatoes, and green beans, and a spinach/mushroom
casserole, and pumpkin and mince and apple pies. A
mixing bowl and beaters wait in the freezer for when it's
time to make the whipped cream.

I actually stood in the grocery store yesterday staring
at a Cornish game hen for a long while before I came
to my senses. So what if I'm alone? So what? I happen
to be having a very good time, yes I am. I'm glad I lied to
my mother, glad I refused Veronica's invitation to have
dinner with her and her boyfriend and told her I was
eating with the neighbors.

I baste the turkey, eat a forkful of stuffing. Oh, it's so
good. I eat another forkful. One more.

Back in the family room, I stretch out on the sofa,
close my eyes. I'm beginning to understand how being
alone can be wonderful. You can do whatever you want!
Travis and David both hate Janis Joplin, for instance.
But now, I can blast her the whole livelong day. Which
I very well might. I put on another one of her CDs,
turn the volume up thrillingly high. I think of the boom-
box man with a new understanding: if someone were to
tell me to turn this down, I too would tell them to fuck
themselves.

After the CD ends, I go into the dining room to lay out
a white linen tablecloth. I set my place with my Tiffany's
china, put candles in the holders. And now I will get
dressed for dinner. Another bath first, even though I was

in the tub for an hour last night with the tabloids. I start the CD over, grab *Vogue*, and head upstairs.

I turn on the water, hot, hot; then sit on the edge of the tub and open the magazine. There is an advertisement featuring a model in gorgeous underwear: diaphanous blue, a pearl here, a bow there. I inspect the woman thoroughly. Well. She is a very lovely girl.

I am not a girl. I am a woman coming into middle age who has had the rug pulled out from under her. And I am trying to reorient myself and I haven't yet. I walk around with ghosts ahead of me and behind me. Pieces of my old life. Pictures of how it used to be: David coming in the front door, home from work. Travis showing him his homework, leaning on the side of David's chair. A movie on Friday night, someone to go with. This is my new life: I push pain away all day, and the moment I put my arms down it walks into me and has a seat.

I undress and stand before the full-length mirror for some time. Then I throw the magazine in the garbage, climb into the tub, lean back, and close my eyes. I take in a deep breath, breathe out. Breathe in again; and then let go. This is not the time in my life to try to look like a model. This is the time in my life to do other things. Janis sings in the family room below me, a song about trying harder.

All right: the red against the blue, the sound of the birds in the morning. The sugar smell in bakeries. The smoothness of fabric moving under my hands into the teeth of the sewing machine. The movement of the ocean, the break of light every morning, every morning.

"Hey," I say softly, just to hear the sound of my own voice. I sit perfectly still, hear the tap drip, then drip again. "Hey!" I yell. "I'm here!"

I begin to soap my legs. And to sing, softly at first; then

loudly. I feel a rush of power that is something like sex. Only better. I start to cry. But this crying, it's so different.

AT FOUR O'CLOCK, I light the candles, then go into the kitchen to load up my plate. Back in the dining room, I sit at the head of the table. David's place. No. Mine. I clear my throat. Spread my napkin on my lap, pick up my fork and knife. And stop. Travis and David and I always used to say three things we were grateful for (one year, Travis said "farting"), but I don't think I want to do that alone. A prayer, then; a type of prayer.

I bow my head, close my eyes. "Thanks," I say. "Thank you." And then, after a long pause, "I know it could be a lot worse." Then, "If you're real . . . If there is something, I hope . . . Well, whatever you are, whatever you may be, thank you for Travis. For all the good I have in my life. Even now."

I open my eyes, spear a piece of white meat that I've drenched in gravy, which is quite the best I've ever made. Next I take a bite of mashed potatoes. Very nice. The green beans, also very good. I reach for the salt, accidentally hit my water goblet with it. The crystal rings, just as it should, and the sound goes on and on. And on.

I go into the family room, turn the radio on to the classical station. There.

Back in the dining room, I stare at my plate. What I really like is the taste of foods mixed together. Well, why not? Who's watching me? Is this not yet another benefit of being alone? I mix my food together, then take a bite. Delicious, but disgusting to look at. Zoo food. Also a little, perhaps, demented.

I go into the kitchen to dump what's on my plate into the garbage disposal. Now I'll start again. I load up my plate once more, sit down at the table, take a few bites, and look around the room.

It's too big in here.

I go to sit at the kitchen table. Much better. Homier. I take another bite, and realize I am full. How many times did I taste that stuffing? I take a deep breath and undo the button to my skirt, which has gotten much too small, try one more bite, but it's no use. I'm just not hungry.

I change into my jeans and clean up, which takes quite a while. The turkey pan, especially. Cleaning up after Thanksgiving should never be done alone. There should be a group of people, chatting—relatives who have known each other for years, husbands and wives who love each other's company, old friends, new friends. Anybody. I should have eaten with my mother and her dumb boyfriend.

I have quite a few leftovers. Enough for thirty, approximately. I can barely fit them into the refrigerator. I never even whipped the cream. For what? I don't want any of the pies I made. I see them lined up on the counter, imagine them looking at each other and shrugging. Then I go out for a walk.

NOTHING IS ON television, Bruce Springsteen is absolutely right; fifty-seven channels, and nothing on. Is it fifty-seven? Maybe it's sixty-seven. It could be six hundred and seven and still nothing would be on. I turn off the television and look at my watch. Eight-thirty. I could go to bed. By the time I got ready, it would be close to nine.

I don't feel like reading. I just finished a novel last night, and after I was done, I stared for a while at the author photo on the back, wishing I could call the woman and say, "I really liked your book. It says here you live with your two daughters. Are you divorced?"

I could call Rita. But why run up the phone bill? I'll see her soon. Besides, Rita's probably busy, having a terrific time, eating dinner with forty creative, California types, all of them mellow, all of them wearing contemporary jewelry and natural fibers and drinking the Napa Valley wines they're so damn proud of. I hate eating with California people when they aren't in California. All they do is talk about their superior produce, as though they are responsible for it, as though I don't know that the only contribution they make is to pull up into the too-clean parking lot of the grocery store in their nonrust *California car!* convertible and fill it with avocados. When they eat in restaurants outside their own state, all they do is say, "In *California*," loudly, as though it's a credit to their personhood that they live there and they need to make sure the waiter and everyone else knows that they do. And why? No seasons, a bunch of airheads running around being so irritatingly happy you wanted to wring their necks. Everybody is happy there. Call directory assistance and you get some ecstatic person, thrilled to death that they live in *California*, they have a job in *California*. Who cares? Who wants to live in California?

Maybe I do.

I sigh, lean back in my chair, close my eyes. How come Rita gets such a good life and I get such a crummy one? How come Rita never has to shovel snow and has a suede checkbook cover? How come Rita's husband adores her, sits lazily in his chair watching her, laughing at all her jokes? Once, when I visited them and the three of us were walking down one of the long, hilly streets of San Francisco, Lawrence turned to Rita and kissed her full on the mouth. Then, turning to me, he said, "I love my wife!"

And I said, "I know you do," feeling too much present, feeling in the way, knowing that David would never do that to me and would in fact object to seeing anyone else do it. "There's a time and a place," he'd say.

How come Rita is a television producer—creative, well paid, well respected; while the apparent outlet for my talents is as proprietress of the Hotel Meatloaf, temporary lodging in a wrecked suburban home? It occurs to me to get out my high school yearbook, to call everyone and say, "I was just wondering. How did things work out for you?" Maybe someone would be in prison, and I could feel better.

I pick up the Martha Stewart catalogue, call the 800 number, ask the woman who answers the phone if she can give me Martha's telephone number. She says, no, sorry, she can't do that.

"I would really like to talk to her," I say. "I need to ask her some things. Of a personal nature."

"I'm sorry, ma'am."

"I went to high school with her," I say. "We were pretty good friends. But we, you know, lost touch."

"I don't have her number," the woman says. "I couldn't give it to you even if I wanted to. Would you like to order something?"

"I wonder . . . would you mind taking my number, and asking her to call me?"

"Surely. What's your number?"

I tell her, then say, "You didn't even write it down, did you?"

"Yes, I did."

Right. "Too bad you have to work on Thanksgiving," I say.

"Oh, I don't mind."

"Do you have to say that?"

"No, I really don't mind."

"Because you know how people talk about Martha, how mean she is."

"*Did* you want to order something?" the woman asks.

"Well, let's see," I say, leafing through the pages. "Anything in here you think is really great?"

"I'll tell you what," the woman says. "Why don't you take a look and then call back?"

I hang up, toss the catalogue aside, look at my watch. Five minutes have passed. Great. I can go to sleep.

Upstairs, I sit gloomily at the edge of my bed. Maybe I should masturbate; probably part of my problem is that I haven't been touched lately. It's terrible not to be touched. I heard about a woman who got divorced and hadn't had sex in three years. She went to a masseuse just to be touched, and she all of a sudden started crying and asked the therapist, "Please, can you just whisper 'I love you' to me?" The worst part of that story is that it was the masseuse who told someone, who then told everyone.

Well, self-love. That's pretty safe. I have the time, God knows. I'm alone, God knows. And it's not a sin; it's not a sin; it's not a sin.

I pull the curtains closed, think of what I might do to make things more interesting. Maybe I'll put on one of the get-ups I used with David. Why not? They're just sitting in the dresser drawer, hidden beneath my socks. If I'm not going to use them, I should give them to the Salvation Army. Wouldn't they have fun, pulling that stuff out of the bin? "Hey, look at *this*!" some guy wearing a hooded sweatshirt would say, holding up one of my silk-and-lace teddies. And another, older, worker would say,

"Yeah, we get that shit all the time. Price it at a buck fifty, buck twenty-five, whatever."

Well, this is not sexy thinking. I should be doing sexy thinking. I dig through my drawer, pull out a red nightgown with a revealing top, a slit high up the side. I undress quickly, then pull the nightgown over my head and get into bed. I'm freezing. This damn nightgown is freezing! Why can't I masturbate in flannel pajamas? Oh, but I can't, I can't do that, it would be like having sex with Mr. Rogers. This nightgown is *sexy*. I just need to wait a minute. I'll warm up. I close my eyes, shiver, rub my hands up and down my arms. There, that's better. And now I open my eyes, look down at my breasts.

Well, there they are, old Mutt and Jeff. Flat as pancakes. I sit up, push them together with the sides of my arms. There. I pull the nightgown up, put my hand to myself, rub gently. Nothing. A fleeting thought of some recipe I saw yesterday in a supermarket cookbook, a casserole that actually looked good, it called for spinach, feta cheese, rice, and . . . lemon, was it lemon?

No. No recipes. Well, what can I think about? Men. Of course, men! I envision a naked man. Not David. A new man, someone I don't know. There he is, there's his nice chest, his fine, muscular arms. Oh, but there's that awful-looking equipment, just hanging there. It is awful looking, women's bodies are so much prettier than men's. That *stuff* men have, just *out* there. The veiny penis, throbbing away in midair as it rises to attention. And those wrinkled testicles, the way they loll about in the hand like warm water balloons. I mean, the very *word* "testicle" is disgusting. Clitoris. That's a nice word. Sounds like a flower. Sounds like your aunt from England, visiting, with tins of butterscotch and yards of grosgrain ribbon.

All right. Concentrate. No testicles. The new man, with a bathing suit on. A blue Speedo, turquoise blue. Nice eyes, nice chest, nice back. Wonderful hands. I close my eyes, rub some more. *Nothing!*

I open my eyes, grimly pull down one side of my nightgown to stare at my naked breast, rub myself again. When I do, my breast shakes a little. It's kind of amusing. And a little grotesque. Which is to say, not sexy.

I lie back down, blow air out of my cheeks, put my hand to myself and rub hard. Harder. Nothing. The hell with it. I'll put on my jeans, go downstairs, and see if I can find an episode of *Father Knows Best*.

AT TEN O'CLOCK, I'm hungry. But I don't want to eat alone. I dial King's number. He answers on the first ring.

"It's me, Sam," I say. "You're home!"

"Yeah, I just got in."

"Did you bring home leftovers?"

"Pardon?"

"Did you bring home leftovers? You know, turkey?"

A long silence and then, "No." And then, "Oh! Right! It's Thanksgiving!"

"Well . . . *yes*. Didn't you go eat dinner somewhere?"

"Yeah. Taco Bell."

"Oh, King, I wish I'd known. I would have invited you to eat with me."

"It's okay. I'm not comfortable eating dinner with a lot of people I don't know. I usually don't even realize it when holidays come around. I get caught up in something, and—"

"It was only me. It would have been only me."

"Oh! Why *didn't* you call me?"

"Well, I thought for sure you'd gone to your parents'. Or somewhere."

"Do you have any leftovers?"

"God, King. Come over, can you?"

"Ten minutes," he says, and then there is a dial tone. Which is the sweetest sound I have heard all day.

Eighteen

FRIDAY NIGHT, I AM BRUSHING MY TEETH BEFORE BED. All of a sudden, I burst into tears. I have a sudden impulse to turn quickly around, to see who is doing this to me. But I'm doing it to myself, I guess. I try ignoring it, take a little walk down the hall with my toothbrush. Tears keep coming, and when I come back into the bathroom and lower my head to spit into the sink, they fall and mix in with the toothpaste. This seems wrong. Unholy. As though the least I could do for myself is to separate the pain from these mundane tasks.

"Sit with your pain," a woman once told me when I was still a student. "Learn from it. It will make you strong." I don't even remember what I was upset about at the time. I don't think that will ever happen with this pain, I don't think I'll ever forget this. Some things make for a psychic limp, and this is one of them.

I go downstairs into the kitchen, open the refrigerator, close it. Go into the family room, turn on the television, turn it off. I go over to the bookshelf to see what movies are there. A lot of Christmas movies. A lot of Disney for Travis. And there, the home movies. Videos of David and Travis and me. I reach for one of those tapes, then put it back on the shelf. And then I take it back out and put it on, wrap up in a quilt, and watch it. Once, I laugh aloud at Travis as an eight-month-old, crawling along the kitchen floor, a bagel in his hand. "Oh, look at that *face*!" I say aloud. To no one. Well, to David. Well, to no one.

Nineteen

RITA IS SITTING ON THE KITCHEN TABLE, HER STOCK-inged feet on a kitchen chair. "I don't know what you're talking about," she says. "I see a *bunch* of good ads in here! Kind of makes me want to start dating, myself." She is looking through a fat booklet of personals we found in an ice-cream store. I'd told her not to bother; there wouldn't be anything good in them. It's so sad, a whole book of people advertising themselves like used cars. And yet I've begun reading them, more and more often.

It's Sunday afternoon. I'm melting butter for popcorn. Then we're going to watch a dirty movie Rita ordered from the back pages of a woman's magazine. *Satin Nights*, it's called, for God's sake. Rita had said she couldn't resist it—"It's made by women for women," she said, "so there won't be any of that Mount Vesuvius stuff the boys love so much." She'd saved it to watch with me. Tonight, King is coming for dinner.

"Here's *another* good one," Rita says.

"Read it to me."

"Okay, listen to this: 'I am forty-five years old, very good-looking, fit, financially secure, interested in someone who can share my joy at Bach and blue jays. I love ball-room dancing, cooking gourmet meals, live theater, rides into the country, antiquing, and honest conversation. Let's be careful with each other, start slow and see where we end up.' " She looks up. "I mean, it's a little dippy, but . . . *nice*. Let's see what else is here."

I watch Rita scanning the column, yanking absent-mindedly at the collar of her sweatshirt. I'm so glad she's here. She makes me remember who I am, *that* I am. I've laughed more these last couple days than I have in the last year. It *is* healing, laughter.

"I *really* like this one," Rita says. "Listen: 'Are you feeling strange about even reading this? I certainly feel strange writing it. But I'm looking for a sincere partner, someone who understands trust and commitment and sensitivity to another's feelings. Looks and age unimportant; soul matters.' "

"Give me that," I say, snatching the booklet away from Rita. I read the ad, stop chewing the popcorn I shoved in my mouth. "Amazing!" I turn the page, read a few more. "Wow, there *are* some good ones in here!" I turn back to see where the ads start. I'll read them all. Finally, I find the bold-faced heading at the beginning of the listings. "Oh," I say, and pass the booklet back to Rita.

She squints at the headline. "MEN SEEKING MEN. Oh. No wonder. Well, let's see what the other ones say, the MEN SEEKING WOMEN."

I pour the butter over the popcorn, mix it with my hands, wince at a hot spot. "I'll tell you what they say. They say, 'I'm an ordinary asshole looking for an extra-ordinary woman to be mean to. Must be beautiful and willing to pick up after me.' "

"Yeah." Rita sighs. "You're probably right." She closes the booklet, pushes it aside. "So forget about men. You don't need them. Start a garden."

"It's too cold."

"Well, send away for catalogues. Start planning one. Just don't go to a therapist, whatever you do."

I sit at the table, put the bowl of popcorn between us. "You sound like my mother. Why not?"

"Oh, I know, everybody goes. But I'm telling you, it's a waste unless you're really nuts. You're better off using the money for something else. Every week, spend a hundred bucks on yourself another way. I know one woman who quit therapy and started doing that. One week she bought a hundred dollars' worth of magazines and brought them to the emergency room of a hospital— she'd been there once and all they had was *Business Week*, you know, *Popular Mechanics*. And then another week she bought a hundred dollars' worth of lipstick."

"Yeah, she probably got two whole tubes."

"No, she went to CVS. She got a whole bunch. She said she tried this bright coral color, which she never would have done otherwise, and it looked fabulous on her, that's all she wears now. She also did this really neat thing: she got four hundred quarters and left them by those machines where you can get gum balls, and rings— you know, those little prizes. And she just left the quarters there with a sign that said, TAKE ONE."

"Well, that was dumb. Someone probably just came along and took all the money."

"No! That's what was so therapeutic about it. She stood around for a long time, watching little kids take just one quarter, then leave the rest. Can you imagine? She said it changed her whole worldview, restored her faith in humanity."

"Well, I hadn't even thought about going to a therapist. But now, seeing that you're so violently opposed to it, I'm thinking maybe I ought to try it."

"Let's watch the movie," Rita says.

I grab the bowl of popcorn, follow her into the family room, watch her bend slightly to slide the cassette into the VCR, then pull back to see better. We've both put off getting bifocals. "Not till the vision police come," she always says.

It's so good to see Rita's sneakers tossed into the corner, her coat hanging in the closet, to know that I can rifle through her purse and ask questions about anything I find. And Rita can look through my purse, too, and my own life will suddenly seem more interesting to me. "That's Travis last summer," I'll say, when Rita comes to his picture in my wallet, and then I'll look at my son over Rita's shoulder, really noticing his T-shirt, really seeing him as the age he is, rather than the usual mix of every age he ever was, mother-vision. No wonder he becomes so exasperated with me. He'll be standing before me in man-sized shoes, arguing rightly to stay up later, and I will look straight into his eleven-year-old face and see him camped out on his potty chair, reading *Goodnight Moon* upside down.

"This thing isn't going in," Rita says, pushing at the tape in the slot. And then, as it slides in smoothly, "Oh. Never mind. There it goes." She turns around, grins. "Now I know how the guy feels."

"Gross," I say, through a mouthful of popcorn.

"Just trying to get you in the mood for the movie." Rita goes to the window to pull the curtains. The late afternoon sun lights up the edges of her bad perm. It really is a bad perm, reminiscent of the fifties' do-it-yourself variety that left your hair looking like you'd had an accident with electricity; Rita said she was thinking about suing the beauty parlor. She's put on weight; her hair looks terrible; but she's still beautiful, still sexy, too.

Now Rita falls into David's recliner, leans back into the full recline position, and presses the remote. "Fasten your seat belt," she says.

The movie opens with a scene of a woman in a garden. Soft-focus blossoms blow in a gentle breeze. The camera focuses on them for so long Rita and I finally look at each other and start laughing.

"Is that *Mozart*?" I ask.

Rita nods, clearly disgusted.

"Fast-forward it," I say, and Rita does. A scene starts where a man dressed in jeans and a flannel shirt is unbuttoning the white blouse of the heroine. "Stop!" I say, and Rita looks at me. "I *know*."

And then we stare straight ahead, eating popcorn, licking salt and butter from our fingers, watching scenes of one kind of nature alternate with another. When the man and woman are taking turns moaning, working tastefully toward the inevitable conclusion, I hear a knock at the door, then see it slowly opening.

"Quick, *quick*!" I tell Rita.

She presses a button, the movie disappears, a football game comes on, and King appears in the family room.

"Hi," he says. "Am I early?" And then, seeing the screen, "Oh. You're watching the Patriots?"

"Who?" I ask.

AFTER DINNER, THE three of us are sitting in the family room again. Travis is upstairs talking on the phone, something he does a lot of lately. I suppose soon I'll have to get him his own line. His own voice mail.

We're talking about David, about why I married him. "Oh, she just did everything too soon," Rita says. "She panicked, and said yes to the first guy that asked her because she was afraid no one better would come along."

I would actually prefer it if Rita didn't broadcast things like this, but one of the things I like most about Rita is her honesty—you just have to take the bad with the good.

"But I'm the one who asked him," I say.

Rita halts her wineglass midway to her mouth. "Really?"

"Well, I mean, we'd talked about it. I was the one to sort of . . . you know, formally *say* it."

"Wow!" Rita says. "I didn't know *that*."

"Well, so what?" I say. "What's the big deal? We'd *talked* about it."

"You know, King," Rita says, "I had to stand by and watch her ruin her life. She was so damn stubborn, shining that ring in my face. I tried to tell her."

"No, you didn't," I say. "I wish you had."

"I did try, right at first. I don't think you even heard me. And then I just gave up. Watched you . . . descend."

"Well, I'm on the rise again." Saying this, I wonder if I believe it. Maybe I do.

"She didn't even *sleep* with anybody else. She didn't—"

"I did, too." I say. "I slept with *nine* guys before David."

Rita shakes her head. "Can you imagine, King? In the early seventies? Nine guys?"

"I don't think nine is so bad," I tell Rita. "How many did you sleep with?"

"Oh, boy. I think I'd need a calculator. Let's see." She sits back, remembering. "It had to be . . . oh, I'd say . . . fifty or so."

"God!" I say.

"That was normal! Don't you think, King? For a woman? I mean, guys did it even more. For a guy, a *hundred* and fifty was probably normal. How many women did you sleep with in the early seventies? If you don't mind my asking."

"In the early seventies?" King asks. "One. One time."

"Oh," Rita says. "Well. But you're . . . you must be a few years younger than we are. So . . . you know, in the late seventies. In the late seventies how many women did you sleep with?"

"None."

We are all quiet, and then King says, "None in the eighties and none in the nineties, either."

"You mean . . . Are you . . . ?" I ask.

"I'm not gay."

"*One* time?" Rita asks, and I have a nearly irresistible impulse to slap her. "Wow! You're practically a virgin!"

King shrugs.

"Rita . . ." I say.

"I don't mind," he says.

A profound silence descends. Finally, King says, "So. Rita. Where exactly in Mill Valley do you live?"

"I CAN'T BELIEVE it!" Rita says, after King leaves and we are in the kitchen washing out the wineglasses. "Have you ever met a guy who hasn't done it a million times? I mean, I know they must be around, but—"

"I think you embarrassed him," I say.

"I didn't embarrass him. He said he didn't mind."

"Maybe he was just being polite."

"That's not it."

"How do you know? You don't even know him."

I rinse out the last glass, start scouring the sink. Rita sits at the table, watching me. "Well, *sorry*," she says. "Although I don't know why I'm apologizing to you."

"I don't, either. He's the one you should apologize to."

"But I don't think he was offended, Sam! He was fine with it. You're the one who's all worked up. Why?"

"Well, maybe it's on his behalf, okay? I mean, he *should* have been offended. You acted like he was a freak or something!"

"No, I didn't! I acted like it was a really unusual thing. Which it is!"

I wipe off the dishwasher door, rinse out the sponge, wipe off the counter. How many days does she have left here?

"You're so *mad*!" Rita says.

"No, I'm not!"

"You are! What in the hell are you so mad about?"

I stop cleaning, straighten, look at her. "I don't know."

A long moment passes. Then Rita says gently, "I mean, come on. Don't you just want to do it with him? You know, teach him some things? 'Yeah, honey; right *there*.' "

Something breaks and I laugh, resume wiping the counter, then move to the stove. "No."

"Really?"

"No! I mean, who needs all that . . . ineptitude?"

Rita shakes her head. "Boy, I would. It would make me feel really powerful."

"Well, you've got five more days here," I say. "Maybe you'll score." I scrub at a stain on the stove that never comes off. And I know it.

Twenty

⬥

MONDAY MORNING, THE BREAKFAST TABLE IS FULL.
Lydia and Rita sit having blueberry pancakes with Travis
while I make more at the stove.

"Why don't you let me cook?" Rita asks. "You need to
go get ready for work."

"It's okay," I say. "I have time." I flip a pancake.
Perfect.

"Come on," Rita says, moving to the stove. "I'm
stuffed. You eat." She takes the spatula from my hand.

I go to the table, drink some orange juice. "I'm sorry I
have to work today."

"I don't mind," Rita says. "I don't need a thing. I want
to just read, relax. Maybe Lydia and I will go out."

"I have a museum tour today," Lydia says. "But you're
welcome to come."

"You can come to school with me," Travis says. "You
can go *instead* of me."

"No thanks," Rita says. "I hate math."

"I hate English," Travis says.

"Yeah, I hate that, too."

"Really?" Travis asks.

"Yeah, I hated everything except gym in school."

"Me, too!" Travis says.

Well, that's it. They're friends for life. Tonight, Travis

will ask to speak with me alone and ask if he can move in with Rita, who will never make him do his homework and who will let him have a tree house. Will let him *build* a tree house with the tools she buys him, including the band saw he found at Sears the other day and spent a good twenty minutes examining, while I stood around in the adjacent hosiery department deliberating over the three hundred thousand kinds of panty hose available. "Will you buy me this?" he'd asked me when I finally came to collect him.

"What is it?"

"A band saw."

"What do you need a band saw for?"

Travis rolled his eyes, then turned for sympathy to a nearby male customer who was lovingly examining torque wrenches. I'd actually looked at the price before I told him no.

I look at my watch, quickly finish a pancake. "I'd better get going. I'll be home pretty early, about two."

"What are you doing today?" Lydia asks.

"Answering phones at a law firm. Receptionist, I guess."

"Don't make coffee!" Rita says. "*Don't make coffee!* Tell them to make their own damn coffee."

"I don't mind making coffee," I say. "Why does everybody hate making coffee so much? I like to make coffee. It's very satisfying. I like the smell. Plus you get to goof off, leave your desk."

"Well, it's a symbol," Rita says. "You don't want them to assume you're there to be their mommy, their wife. That's what they do to women."

"It's an all-woman law firm," I tell her.

"Oh," Rita says. "Well. Bring in some gourmet grounds, then. And a dozen donuts."

"Just what I need," I say, patting my stomach. I weighed myself this morning. I'm nine pounds up. Pretty soon my robe belt will be too short.

AT TWO-THIRTY, I let myself in the kitchen door, call out hello. I feel bad that I'm half an hour late. But I wanted to stop for groceries. Lasagna, we'll have tonight. I'll put some spinach in there so I'll feel virtuous. And Lydia has promised to make her famous caramel apple pie.

I put the bag of groceries on the counter. "Hello?" I yell again.

Nothing. I go to the bottom of the stairs, yell, "Rita?" And then, "Lydia?" Nothing.

They must have gone somewhere together. Well, that's good. Now Rita will see what I like so much about Lydia, she'll see what a great choice she was for a roommate. Although she will be gone soon, she and Thomas are getting married in two weeks. I sigh, thinking about it. I really should find another roommate to take Lydia's place. The rent from Ms. Blue won't be enough. And besides, she's too quiet, and too weird—she's gone a lot, and when she's home, she stays by herself in the basement almost all the time. I want someone who'll be good to talk to, as Lydia was. I've had a sign up in a few places for a few days, but there have been no calls yet.

I'm putting the last of the groceries away when the door opens, and Rita comes in with King. "Hey!" Rita says, her eyes wide, her cheeks flushed.

Oh my God, she did it. She slept with him.

"Hey, Rita," I say, evenly. "Hi, King."

He nods at me, unwinds his scarf from around his neck. "We were ice-skating. At the rink, you know, that rink off Ninety-four?"

"Yeah, I know it. You didn't have to work today?"

"No, tonight. Security, at the mall. Do you want to go skating? We came back to get you and Travis."

"No, I . . . don't skate."

"We don't either!" Rita says. *We.* "That's why it's so great! We spent all our time on our butts."

"I don't think so. But if *you* guys want to go back, it's okay. Just go."

I see Rita and King exchange glances, and then Rita says, "Actually, I think I've had about enough."

King looks at me, then wraps the scarf back around his neck. "Yeah, I've got some errands . . . I'll see you later, Sam."

I nod tightly.

"Good-bye, Rita."

She goes to the door, hugs him. "I loved meeting you."

I'll bet she did. I pull a pan out of the cupboard. "Want lasagna for dinner?"

"What's the matter, Sam?"

"*What?* I just wanted to know if you wanted lasagna for dinner!"

"Are you mad about something? Again?"

I get out the olive oil, the garlic.

"Come on, Sam. It's me."

I look at her. "I just . . . he's my new friend. And you're . . ."

"What? Wearing him out? Using him up? I'm *sorry,* he called here looking for you; I didn't have anything to do . . ."

"It's okay," I say. "I'm just tired. Forget it." He called looking for *me.*

"Let's eat out," Rita says. "All of us. My treat. Really, I wanted to take you all out at least one night. Let's do it tonight."

"All right." I come over to the table, sit down. "Rita? You didn't try to seduce him, did you?"

"Oh, Sam." She leans over, starts tugging at her boots. "Jesus."

"Well, remember you were saying how powerful it would make you feel? How you wanted to—"

"Yes. I remember."

"So, tell me the truth, now. Did you try?"

She stares off to the side, considering. "Well, no. I mean, I didn't *really* try."

"What did you do?"

"I just . . . I asked him if he wanted to do it."

Cartoonlike, my mouth falls open. I knew it.

"But I wasn't really serious!"

"Weren't you?"

"Well . . . *no*! I mean, if he'd said yes, I—"

"What? What would you have done?"

"Well, I don't know! I mean, maybe I *would* have done it."

I sit back in my chair, stunned. "What about Lawrence?"

"Oh, Sam. We've been married a long time."

"What do you *mean*?"

"Well, fifteen years. That's a long time, don't you think?"

"I don't mean how many years!" I say. "I mean . . . well, what do *you* mean? You're married for a long time, so it's okay to have affairs?"

"This wouldn't be an affair, Sam! It would be . . . you know, a friendly *gesture*, that's all! A public service. Well, a private service."

"What about . . . disease?" This is not what I mean. Not at all.

"He's all but a *virgin*, Sam."

"And God knows *you're* not."

A beat. And then Rita says, "I'll just let that go, Sam. I think you know me well enough to know . . . Look. He didn't want to. And anyway, *you're* not interested in him that way! Are you?"

"*No!* I *told* you!"

"Yeah," Rita says slowly. "That's what you said." And then, as Travis comes in the door, home from school, "Hey, buddy. Where would you like to go out for dinner?"

"A place *not fancy*!" Travis says.

"My man," Rita answers.

AT THE AIRPORT, Rita hugs me so hard it hurts. "I'm sorry," she says. "This was not a good visit. I'm a bad person."

"You're not a bad person. You're just pathologically honest. Most of the time I like it. But it's still a tense time for me. You know. I'm still sort of nuts. I miss David, I hate David . . . I guess I take it out on everyone."

"Do you really want him back?"

"I'm supposed to say no, right?"

"You're supposed to say the truth."

"Well . . . I don't know. In some ways, my life is better now. But David . . . Oh, I know you hated him. But I still feel so attracted to him. Or attached. Or something."

Rita looks at her watch, picks up her briefcase. "I know. I understand."

"No, you don't."

"Look, I think you're doing fine. I like your life now. It seems . . . truer. More honest. I like your roommate, I like your friends."

"King, you mean."

"Yeah, King. And I wouldn't *really* have—"

"I know."

"Did I tell you his pants fell down at the skating rink?"

"What! No, you didn't tell me that!"

"Well, probably because it was so . . . you know, when I came home. But yeah, his pants fell down! Right in the middle of the rink!"

"You probably pulled them down," I say.

"No, come on, it was just . . . spontaneous! It wasn't too bad, because his coat was long enough to, you know, mostly cover him. And he yanked them back up again really fast. I fell down again, I was laughing so hard."

"Was he embarrassed?"

"I guess a little. But I don't think too many people saw. His pants were just too big. He's losing weight, you know. Over twenty pounds, so far."

"Yeah, I thought so." His face looked a little different, last time I saw him, especially around the eyes.

The final boarding call for Rita's flight is announced. "I'll call you," she says, walking toward the Jetway. "All the time."

"I know."

"I'm glad I came."

"Me, too."

"I'm wearing my new shirt tomorrow," she calls. "You wear yours."

"Okay." We'd bought matching blue flannel shirts. An old tradition: each time one of us visits the other, we buy something alike. I wonder what we'll buy in our eighties. I can see us standing together in some department-store aisle, holding up flannel nighties for each other's shaky inspection. Probably asking each other if the gowns make us look fat.

I watch at the window as Rita's plane takes off. It heads in one direction for a while, then reverses itself as though it has just changed its mind.

Twenty-one

LATE SATURDAY MORNING, I AM IN THE BASEMENT CUTting out pieces of fabric for a quilt I'm making for Travis. It's a simple nine-patch, but I'm making it with the softest flannel I could find, in muted, masculine colors. It's going to be beautiful. The phone rings and I ignore it. Then I hear Travis calling, saying it's for me. "Can you take a message?" I call back.

A moment. And then he comes downstairs to say, "It's Martha Stewart."

I stare at him blankly, the scissors in my hand.

"Did you hear me?"

"I . . . *Yes!*"

"She's the one everybody makes fun of."

"*Shhh!*"

"She can't hear me!"

I go upstairs into the kitchen, and then it comes to me who's really calling.

"Hi, Rita." I say. "Very funny."

"Pardon?" an unfamiliar voice says.

"Oh! Sorry, I thought . . . This is Samantha Morrow."

"Yes, I know. I called *you*. This is Martha Stewart."

"Well, I . . . I . . ."

"I had a message saying that we went to high school together, and you needed to talk to me?"

"Oh, no, I just . . . I was . . . Well, it was a bad day, you know, and I just wanted to talk to you. I don't know why. I'm sorry. We didn't go to high school together."

"I'm well aware of that."

Travis, who has been standing beside me, whispers loudly, "*Is* it her?"

I nod, motion for him to go away. He doesn't.

"So what can I do for you, Samantha?"

"Oh, it's . . . 'Sam.' "

"All right. Sam, then."

I look at Travis, who looks pointedly away, then turn my back to him. "Well, Martha, I just . . . I actually wanted to ask you some questions about . . ." I clear my throat. "Can you hold on for one second, please?" I turn to Travis, and in a dangerous whisper say, "Go up to your room for a while. Now."

He frowns, runs upstairs, and I hear his door slam.

"Sorry," I say. And then, "You know, Martha, I just want to say that it's so nice of you to call. I've had this fantasy . . . I wanted to ask you some things about divorce. I—"

"Are you a reporter?"

"Me? Oh no, I'm nothing."

"You're nothing?"

"Well, I mean, I'm . . . I just wanted to ask you if you . . . kind of . . . fell apart after your divorce, Martha. That's what I wanted to ask you. I thought if even you did, I could—"

"I don't think that's something I'd like to discuss."

"Oh, I know. I know. I'm sorry. I'm so embarrassed."

"Is that all you wanted?"

"Yes. Although, as long as I have you on the phone . . . I'm making a quilt, out of flannel? For my son? The one who answered the phone? And I was wondering about the backing, whether to use gray flannel or red."

"How old is he?"

"Eleven."

"Gray. Red trim. What pattern are you using?"

"A nine-patch."

"Good. Make sure you use a little yellow right next to the gray."

"Yes, I have some in there. A yellow plaid."

"And on the back, put one square on the lower right-hand corner."

"Oh, what a good idea! I will! Thank you."

"I've got to be off, now."

"Martha, before you go, I just want to tell you that I once met a man at a party, a psychiatrist, a very attractive man, who said that he wanted to marry you."

"I see."

"Really, he was very attractive."

"Well, thanks for telling me."

"Okay. Thank *you*!"

"Samantha?"

She said my name. "Yes?"

"I didn't fall apart. I spent one evening with Bernstein's *Kaddish* and a bottle of 'eighty-six Montrachet. And then I got busy. Try it."

A click. I sit at the kitchen table, think who this might really have been. But it sounded like her.

Travis comes back downstairs, sits with me at the table.

"Were you eavesdropping?" I say.

"No!"

"Just a little?"

"Well, God, Mom, it was Martha Stewart! She's practically a celebrity!"

"Don't say 'God,' Travis."

He rolls his eyes. "Well, *gee*, it was—"

"And she *is* a celebrity."

"Not really, 'cause everybody hates her."

"Not everyone. And anyway, we don't really know who it was." I head back down to the basement. Gray backing. One patch, lower right-hand side. Joke or not, something is occurring to me. You live your life, and you get to ask for things, and sometimes they are given to you.

JUST BEFORE BED, the phone rings. After I say hello, I hear my mother shrieking, "Martha Stewart called you?" Travis. I wonder who else he told. David? I hope he told David.

"It was probably a joke."

"Oh, I don't think it was a joke. I hear she doesn't have much of a sense of humor."

"Ma. I don't think it was really *her*."

"Oh. Who would it be, then?"

"I don't know."

"Well, I think it *was* her. And it only goes to show you."

"Fine. Right."

Twenty-two

THOMAS LIFTS LYDIA'S VEIL ALMOST EXACTLY AS I HAD imagined it, then kisses her with great tenderness. My eyes well up in a mix of longing and despair, my usual re-action to weddings, only worse. I reach down for my purse so that I can get some Kleenex, and notice Travis drawing on his hand. A game of ticktacktoe, apparently. I put my hand over his, shake my head no. He sighs, looks at me wide-eyed. I can nearly hear what he's think-ing: *It's so boring! Just let me draw! Why can't I just draw?* I stare back, stone-faced, until he puts the pen back in his suit pocket. For the first time, I wish he were with his father. But this is my weekend. David is away. He gave me a New York City number—for *emergencies.* Museums, I imagine, the two of them walking hand in hand. Dinners, plays. A nice hotel room, a view of the park.

Travis doesn't perk up much at the reception, either, even when he dances with Marie. I finally give up, say my good-byes, and march Travis out to the car. Snow is falling lazily, fat flakes that look like cut-up pieces of lace.

For a long while, we say nothing. The wiper blades squeak and flop, squeak and flop. Finally I say, "I'm very disappointed in the way you behaved, Travis. You like Lydia. And you like Thomas. This was their *wedding*!

That's a very important day. They deserved more from you."

He turns on the radio, and I turn it off.

"Jesus Christ," he mutters.

"Oh, my God! Don't you dare say that again! And I would appreciate the courtesy of a reply from you. I'm trying to talk to you."

"You're yelling at me."

"I'm not yelling."

"Yes, you are. On the inside, you are."

Well. He has a point.

"Oh, Travis, I just . . . Didn't you find it . . . moving?"

He says nothing.

"Travis?"

"What?"

"I asked you a question."

"You'll just get mad if I tell you what I thought."

I stop at a light, look over at him. "Tell me."

"I thought it was dopey, okay? I mean, aren't they embarrassed?"

I smile. "Why should they be embarrassed?"

"Because they're like . . . old!"

"And?"

"What do you *mean*?" he asks, exasperated.

"I mean so *what* if they're old?"

"Well, you know! It just looks stupid seeing her all in a *bride* dress and everything."

The car behind us honks, and I move forward. *Choose your battles*, I'm thinking. *Wait until he forgets his wife's birthday. Then spank him.*

"Anyway," Travis says, "you shouldn't be allowed to get married twice."

Ah.

"You shouldn't be allowed to get married twice?"
I say.

"No."

"Well, what if your husband dies?"

He says nothing, stares sullenly ahead.

"Lydia's husband was dead, Travis."

"Yeah," he says. "But you're not."

I look quickly at him. "Is . . . Did Dad say something?
About getting married again?"

"I don't know."

"Travis? Did he?"

"I don't *know*!" He punches on the radio. "Just let me
listen to this, okay? I don't want to talk!"

"All right," I say. "That's fine." I don't want to talk
anymore right now, either. Not to Travis. And oh, not to
David, either. I don't want to hear it until I have to.

Twenty-three

MY MOTHER DECLINES A REFILL OF COFFEE, AND ASKS
for the check. We are out to lunch, where she has just
told me she's been asked by Jonathan's father to apologize to me on behalf of his son. To apologize and to ask if
I might perhaps be willing to give it another go.

"No," I say. "No way." I drain my Coke glass. *"Absolutely not."*

"Maybe next Saturday night?"

"Jesus, Ma. Please. You don't know what happened."

"Well . . . what *did* happen?"

"I don't want to see that vile man again, ever. Ever."

She stares at me, and I stare back. "Maybe in a few
weeks," she says, finally, and then digs in her purse for
her compact. She freshens her lipstick, adjusts the curls
at the side of her face. Then, "So! Lydia's wedding was
nice, huh?"

"It was beautiful."

"I wonder what it's like to get married late in life."

"Why?" I say. "Are you thinking about getting married again?" *Oh, God.*

"Am *I* thinking about it? Oh, no. No."

"Well, why not? You were happy the first time around,
right?"

"Yes, I was. Very happy. But I don't expect that kind of

174

thing could happen again. You know, before you girls were born, your father and I would have the most wonderful weekends. We'd just . . . talk. Read . . . Listen to the radio at night and dance. We'd never answer the phone, either. It was so peaceful."

"And then we came along and you had to answer the phone?"

"Well, of course, honey. You know that. When children come, you have to answer the phone. And . . . everything. They come first. But you *want* them to. You want to take care of them. Right?"

"Right." A memory comes to me of being lifted out of the car by my father. It was late at night, we'd just arrived home, and I was pretending to be asleep. I was seven, too old to be carried, really, and thus vastly appreciative of it. My father pushed the front seat out of the way to reach in for me. I remember peeking out at the outline of his hat against the night sky, his open coat being blown away from the tweed suit that always carried the smell of his pipe tobacco. "Maybe we should just wake her up," my mother whispered worriedly, as my father struggled to get me into his arms. "Your back, darling."

"Shhh!" he whispered. "Let her sleep."

"Ha! *She's* not asleep!" Louise said. "I'll bet you ten million *dollars* she's not asleep. Look, she's *smiling*!"

"No, she's not," my father said, and I felt him looking down into my face which was, in fact, smiling. "She's sound asleep," he said, and I smiled bigger.

"I still miss Daddy sometimes," I say.

"Do you, honey? Do you remember him well?"

"Yes. I mean, I think so. I remember, at least, how it felt, when he was there. And I knew you loved him very much, Mom."

"Yes. I sure did. You know how I first knew?"

I shake my head.

"The first time I ironed one of his shirts. Honestly! He'd come to pick me up for a date. We were going to the movies, I remember—something starring Joan Crawford. And he'd had a little mishap, I think he'd spilled water on himself, but anyway, his shirt was all wrinkled. Well, I said I'd iron it. And of course Grandma was all upset that a man would be taking a *shirt* off in her house, but he was very gentlemanly, he always was, and he went in the bathroom and he handed me his shirt through the crack in the door. I liked that he would give me his shirt like that. It seemed so personal. It seemed like he trusted me. And when I ironed it, I got this . . ." She looks at me, smiles. "Well, I guess you're old enough to know this, now. My God, Sam. You're forty-two years old!"

"Yes, I *know* that."

"I just can't believe it!"

"Well, believe it, it's true. But what happened, when you ironed his shirt?"

"Oh. Well, I got this kind of . . . *sexy* feeling, you know? I remember I started with the sleeves, and I wanted them to be perfect, so I was ironing very carefully. And all of a sudden I felt so *good*, way down in my stomach. Then I ironed the top part, where his shoulders went, and . . . .oh, Lord!" She closes her eyes, smiles. "Well. Anyway, I had the feeling that there was nothing I'd rather be doing at that moment than ironing this man's shirt. And that's when I knew. *The man I love,* I was thinking. And him just sitting there in the little bathroom in his undershirt, waiting for me to finish so he could put it on. Why, it just *sent* me!" She laughs out loud. "I know that, to you, this must sound very foolish."

"No, it doesn't," I say. There *is* something in it, the simple act of doing a favor for the one you love. I remember returning a library book for a boy I was crazy about in high school. I liked thinking that his hands had been on the pages, and I liked handing the book to the librarian thinking, For you. From him. Through me.

The truth is, I like any evidence of love between people. I know there are those who thrive on living alone, but how? How, when they know that the cereal box will empty only when they finish it; when they walk into a house where, rather than the mixed evidence of life lived together, there is only the quiet imprint of one? I have brown hair, I am right-handed, I can curl my tongue, and I must have someone to love.

Veronica puts on her coat, and we head for the door. "Any prospects for a roommate yet?"

"One, finally. I'm going to interview him Saturday."

" 'Him'?"

"It's all right. He's gay."

"Oh my Lord." She stops walking.

"Let's go," I say. "We'll talk all about how terrible it is if I decide to let him move in. But I need someone, soon."

I get into the car, think about how this morning, I stood in Lydia's empty room, wondering who could live here now. I need someone who isn't a mistake, as Lavender Blue turned out to be. The girl is profoundly depressed. Lately, she ventures out of her room only to eat and to go to the bathroom. When she offered last week to start teaching Japanese to Travis, something we'd initially agreed upon to help reduce the rent, I declined. I feared for his worldview, should he spend much time with her.

Recently, she told me that in her opinion, life was nothing but one major disappointment after the other. She'd leaned forward, hands wrapped around the cup of cocoa I made for her, thinking we were finally going to have a pleasant getting-to-know-you chat, just like Anna and the king's children. Instead, the girl sat with her spiky blond hair and vacant eyes, staring over my shoulder and talking in a near-monotone. "It's like when I was a little girl and I wanted so much to go on a pony ride. I kept asking my parents to take me on one. I thought I'd be wearing fringe and a cowgirl hat and the horse would be so clean and pretty—a palomino—and it would be prancing and all its decorations would be jingling and I'd be so tall and straight, holding the reins and galloping away. But then when I finally went it was just some sad old brown horse in this crummy field and a man in a T-shirt with greasy hair was leading it around by a clothesline. And every few steps the pony would stop and blow stuff out of his nose and then the man would have to hit him to get him going again. And I saw right away that that's how life was going to be. False promises. Just . . . black. I'm writing a poem about it for my English class. It's called 'Truth in the Ring.' " She sighed, blew on her cocoa, looked up at me. "You know what I mean? Like I am so *on* to life. There's nothing good coming my way." There were dark circles under her eyes, a tender pimple starting on her chin.

"Well, I know I sometimes felt that way," I said. "I mean, when I was your age. But Lavender . . ." I leaned forward, smiled. "You know, I wonder if . . . Did you say your real name was Elaine?"

"Yeah."

"Would you mind if I called you that?"

"Yeah, I'd mind. I hate *Elaine*. That's why I changed it to something to suit me. Lavender Blue, that suits me."

"All right," I said. "It's just that . . . Well. What I wanted to tell you, is that it gets better. Life. It does!"

"Are *you* happy now?"

I started to answer, then stopped.

"See? Anybody who tells the truth would have to say that they're not. Nobody's happy. Not really. Not for any length of time."

"Well," I said. "I—"

"It's okay," Lavender said. "I'm used to it. So! Good night!"

I GO TO bed early and then suddenly awaken. It's seven minutes after eleven. I stare at the ceiling, sigh. Then I pull the phone under the covers with me and call David. He answers after three rings, his voice husky.

"I'm sorry, were you sleeping?" I ask.

"No. It's fine. What's up?"

This is what he says when he wants to hurry people, *What's up?* He used to look at me when he said it to someone else on the phone, rolling his eyes.

"I need to ask you something," I say. "Did you happen to say anything to Travis about getting married again?"

"About getting married again?"

Stalling. This is what he always does when he's uncomfortable with a question, repeats it back to me.

"Yes, about getting married again."

"No, I didn't say anything. It was more . . . Well, I think maybe Vicky was just talking about the notion of people getting married, *generally,* and he must have thought she and I had been talking about it."

"Had you been?"

"Oh, not . . . You know, just in the most general of ways."

"As in . . . ?"

He sighs. "Sam? I don't think this is an appropriate discussion for us to be having. Suffice it to say I don't have any plans for remarriage right away."

"I would think not, since you're not divorced yet."

"I'll let you know. Anything you need to know, I'll let you know."

"Is she there?"

Silence.

"Is she?"

A sigh. "I don't really think that's any of your business."

I feel socked in the stomach. Because he is right.

"I just wanted to talk to her. I just wanted to tell her it's probably not a good idea to be talking to Travis about marrying his father."

"She knows that."

"Apparently not."

"Sam—"

"I don't want to hear it, David. Just . . . Get smart, you know? And tell your girlfriend to get smart, too."

"Was there anything else?"

"No. There was nothing else."

"All right. Good night."

I hang up the phone. Swallow. Swallow again. I hate that he will now tell Vicky that it was me on the phone. There they are, lying together. She's seen every part of his body. I turn on the bedside light. Turn it off.

I walk over to the window and look out at the back-yard. A couple of inches of snow out there. The bird feeders, empty. The bare rhododendron bushes, all those black branches. But in the spring, they will bloom. And in the summer, who will mow the lawn? I lean my fore-head against the glass, and in the fog that my breath leaves behind, write my initials.

Twenty-four

"HELLO, MRS. *GIBBONS*?" I SAY.

"Yes?" The woman's voice on the other end of the line is guardedly suspicious.

"This is Mrs. *Morrow*," I say, as I've been instructed ("'Mrs.' makes them trust you more. Use Mrs. even if you're Miss, any questions about that?"). Then, turning to my script, I say, "I'm calling from the customer *service* desk at *Supersave*."

This is not true. I am calling from First Rate Home Delivery Food Service. For the last four days, I've been working as a telephone solicitor, sitting in a blue folding chair at a kind of Formica counter, in a row of other solicitors. There are five booths on each side of the small room, but only three solicitors are here today, as has been true every other day that I've been here. A thick piece of perforated particle board separates the booths from each other. I've spent a fair amount of time looking thorough the holes at pieces of the person beside me, a busty older woman with blue rhinestone glasses who wears pleated skirts, sheer ruffled blouses, and an excess of a perfume I think might be Youth Dew. She reminds me of a kindergarten teacher turned hooker.

The woman seems to dislike me for reasons I have not been able to discover, yet insists on taking the booth beside me every day. So I peer through the holes at her while I wait for people to answer their phones, looking for some kind of evidence as to why the woman feels the way she does. So far I've figured out nothing except that the woman has an earwax problem, which probably accounts for the many times a day she practically screams, "Pardon me? Can you speak up? I think there's something wrong with your phone!"

The other full-time solicitor is a skinny, gray-haired man who smells like beer and hovers hunch-shouldered over his phone, as though it is a lover he has backed into the corner for a kiss. Every day thus far, he has worn a white shirt with the sleeves rolled up, and shiny, navy blue pants, belted too high. Periodically, he coughs for a good long while, finishing with a spectacular hawking of phlegm into a handkerchief that he then stuffs back into his pocket.

The office is located over a dry cleaners, and I can hear the muted sounds of the workers below talking to each other in Spanish, and laughing. I'm jealous of them. I'm not having any fun at all. I've been in that dry cleaners, never knowing that this office was above it, much less that I'd someday be working in it. It's a very pleasant dry cleaners, clean and bright, flowering plants in pretty, woven baskets on the counter, tastefully framed reproductions on the wall. Here, the sunlight pushes in through filthy windows onto a cracked linoleum floor. There is a stained coffee urn in the corner, a half-dead corn plant next to it.

"Now, you recently entered a *contest* to win a *free* side of *beef*, is that right?" I ask my customer.

"*Yes?*"

"Well, the *drawing* for that prize will be held next week," I say.

"Ohhhhh," the woman says. "I thought I won!"

"No, the *drawing* for that prize will be held next week. But I'd *also* like to tell you, Mrs. Gibbons, that *First Rate Home Delivery Food Service* is offering a *free*, *week's* supply of *vegetables* for allowing our salesman to *visit* you in your *home*. He will explain how you can save *time* and *money* by having frozen food *delivered* to you. Now, the reason for *my* call is to determine the *best time* for our salesman to *call*."

Silence.

"Mrs. Gibbons?"

"Yeah?"

"I was wondering when would be the *best time* for our salesman to *call*?"

"Oh, I don't know." The woman sighs. "I don't know. I guess seven-thirty, something like that."

"Seven-thirty this evening?"

"I guess."

"Fine!" I say. "And you live at 311 Walnut Street?"

"Yes," the woman says, and then, lower, "Oh boy, my husband's going to kill me."

"Pardon?"

"I said, my husband's going to kill me. He don't like salesmen."

"Oh, is that right?"

"Yeah, especially when they come to your house. You know."

"Yes, I understand."

"But you say I get a free week's supply of vegetables?"

"Yes, you do." I'm getting nervous now. There is no script for this.

"What kind of vegetables?"

"I think . . . Actually, it's just some frozen vegetables. Three boxes. Corn, green beans, and something else. I think maybe lima beans."

"That don't sound like a week to me."

"Well, they're big boxes."

"Plus I don't like lima beans."

"I don't either," I say. "But I hear they're good in some kinds of soup."

"Well, is it Green Giant or anything?"

"No. It's actually First Rate brand."

"Is that good?"

"I haven't really, you know, tasted them," I say. "I've only seen the boxes. They look nice, though. There's a picture of a cornfield on the corn box. It's probably good."

"Oh." The woman breathes into the phone, then says, "*Thank* you, honey."

"Pardon?"

"I'm sorry—I was talking to my son. He just handed me something." I hear the throaty babble of a very young child.

"How old is he?" I ask.

"Eighteen months." I can hear the smile in the woman's voice, and am suddenly in the woman's kitchen with her, leaning against the counter, drinking coffee, and watching the boy. His hands are holding on to his mother's pants leg. Graham-cracker crumbs are in the curls of his fine, bright hair. Bells are on his shoes.

"Into everything, huh?" I ask, remembering Travis as a toddler, sitting stunned-looking as I screamed and grabbed plant fertilizer away from him. He hadn't yet eaten it, and I burst into tears of relief, which caused Travis to burst into tears as well. We consoled each other, me by holding him tightly, he by being not dead.

"Oh, you wouldn't *believe* it," the woman says. "He's broke our toilet three times already, throwing things down it. Last time, we were flat out of money, couldn't call a plumber for a week. We had to use the neighbor's. You can imagine."

"Oh, I can."

"So anyway . . . you say your salesman will be here at seven-thirty?"

Oh yeah, I think, and look down at my script.

"Yes, that's right, seven-thirty."

"Could I just ask you something?" the woman says.

"Sure."

"Do I have to do this?"

"Well . . . No. Of course not."

"Will I still be entered for the side of beef, though?"

"Absolutely."

"Okay, so can you just, you know, take my name off your list or whatever? My husband would just kill me anyway."

"Sure. That's fine. Well, you have a good day, Mrs. Gibbons. And kiss that baby."

I hang up the phone, tear the lead sheet up, throw it in the garbage. And then feel the presence of someone behind me. It is my supervisor, a balding, pit-faced man, somewhere in his late fifties, I think, who takes his job very seriously. "May I see you in my office, Ms. Morrow?" he asks.

I follow him into the tiny room. "Close the door, will you?" he says.

I sit at the edge of the chair in front of the man's desk, fold my hands in my lap. He sits down heavily, puts his hands behind his head, leans back in his chair. He looks out the window for some time, then turns to me. "You're fired, lady."

"Oh, I know," I say. "I don't blame you a bit."

"I mean, you don't seem to *understand* this job."

"I know. You're right." I pick up my purse.

"You call these people and have a little *chat*! You're not here to chat. You're here to read the *script*, get *leads*! You've gotten one lead in four days!"

"Uh . . . yes, that's right." I take a quick look at the door. He doesn't have to talk so loudly. I'll bet everyone can hear. They've probably even stopped work in the dry cleaners and are standing motionless, looking up at the ceiling.

"Look," I say. "I know I'm really, really terrible at this. If I were you, I'd fire me, too." I stand, smooth my skirt. Smile. "So! If you don't mind, I'll just—"

"I heard that on Tuesday you were recommending dentists to someone, Ms. Morrow."

"Yes, well . . . That's right. That did come up. With someone." I realize now why Youth Dew sits next to me.

"What's the problem, anyway? You seem like an intelligent woman. What's so *difficult* about this job?"

I sit back down. "You want to know what's difficult about it? It's lying. It's lying! I mean, I'm not calling from Supersave!"

"That's where we got their number. Close enough."

"And the people think they *have* to let the salesman come. I have to say *when* can he come, not *can* he come."

"Because if you ask if he *can* come, they'll say no."

"Right," I say, leaning forward. "And see? Why do this? Why not just be honest, say right out what it is that you're offering. You know, you could just call people and describe your service over the phone honestly and see if they want to sign up. Over the phone! You wouldn't even need salesmen to go out. You'd probably save a lot of money."

The man sits up, folds his hands on his desk, and looks at me over the top of his glasses. Shakes his head. "Go home. I'll pay you for today. But don't come back tomorrow, all right?" He picks up a stack of papers, begins reading.

"Yes, well, all right. Thank you."

He doesn't even look up.

LATER THAT NIGHT, with everyone in the house asleep, I wrap myself in the quilt on the sofa and call King. "I got fired today," I tell him.

"Oh yeah? From what?"

"I was doing telephone soliciting."

"Where?"

"First Rate Foods."

"Overdressed dowager and man with consumption?" King asks.

"Yes!"

"Yeah, I've been there. Got fired myself."

I uncurl my legs, sit up straight. "Really! Why?"

"Not enough leads."

"Me, too!"

"There you go. Be proud! It's good to get fired every now and then. It's liberating. Gives you some time during the week to run errands."

"But . . . I need to work."

"The agency won't care. They'll give you more work."

"They will?"

"Hell, yes."

"Oh."

Silence. And then, "Well . . . thanks, King."

"You're welcome."

I hang up and lean back against the cushions, my shame transformed into satisfaction. It lies across my chest like a cat.

Maybe I'll scramble some eggs. Reward myself.

Twenty-five

"I ADMIT IT," EDWARD SAYS. "IN MANY WAYS, I'M A walking cliché. But I'm very comfortable with that. I know my own self. I'm a good person and I have nothing to apologize for." He is sitting at my kitchen table, handsomely dressed in tweed pants and a beautiful cream-colored shirt, one long leg crossed over the over, sipping coffee. He reminds me of a young Fred Astaire: a thin, narrow face, hair looking as though it will recede a bit farther if you turn your back. When Edward talked about knowing himself, he laid his hand over his heart. I like people who do that. I feel I can trust them.

"Well, King certainly speaks highly of you," I say.

Edward rolls his eyes. "Is he a *doll*? I just love him. He's really very handsome, you know. Under all that . . . sort of . . . flesh. Every time I cut his hair, I think, boy what a little weight loss would do."

"He has lost some. Quite a bit, actually."

"Yes, I *thought* so. But I'm talking about . . . I mean, can't you just see him in a Gucci ad?"

I smile.

"Oh, I know," Edward says, "I have a very good imagination. My mother used to get after me all the time for lying on my bed and dreaming up things instead of going outside to grow big and strong and heterosexual. She was sort of like Bette Davis: The Later Years, only she was like that all her years."

"Really?"

"Oh yeah, she used to come in my room and scare my friend Martin Harris to death. I think we were in love with each other, but it was only fourth grade. She didn't like him, of course—he took ballet, for one thing. She'd open the door and there would be her pop-out eyes and this really magnificent scowl. Red lipstick. She'd be holding a cigarette with her arm bent up, big chunky bracelet, and she'd take this incredibly deep drag and say"—here Edward lowered his voice—" 'What are you boys up to? Is this any way to spend a beautiful day?' and then she'd exhale for about an hour and a half. So we'd go outside for a few minutes and then come back in and play dolls with our soldiers." He shrugs. "But you had to like her, you know? I mean, I *liked* her."

"Edward," I say. "I hope you don't mind my asking this. But why would you want to live here?"

"I don't mind your asking. I like families. I don't like living alone. And I don't like living in . . . the Community. It's just a little too intense."

"Oh?"

"Oh, sure."

Silence.

Well, fine, I'm dying to know, but if he doesn't want to tell me . . .

"You could get back to me," he says. "I know the idea is a bit unusual. I will tell you, though, I'm a very good roommate. I clean, I cook, I'm quiet. And I'm . . . entirely discreet. Plus I'll cut your hair for free. I think, if you don't mind my saying so, you could use some color, too."

My hand flies to my hair. "Really? The gray?"

Edward nods solemnly.

"It's really obvious?"

He nods vigorously.

"Well, I don't mind it. I mean, it's natural. It's what happens, you know, when you get older."

"Honey, you can have gray hair when you're sixty. For now, you're much too young and attractive. I'd use a dark brown base, then a little copper for highlights. It would make your eyes look greener."

I nod, think for a moment. "Okay, I'll let you know."

Edward gathers up his coat, stands. "You can call me whenever you like. And I'll understand if you can't let me move in."

"Oh, no. I mean, I'll think about the hair color. You can move in on the first."

He sits down again. "Really?" His happiness is so dear, so transparent. We sit for a moment, smiling shyly at each other. And then Edward says, "But don't you think you should, you know, check me out? Call my references?"

Oh. I should probably do that. But why? What would he do, give me bad references? "No need," I say.

Edward takes a folded paper from his man's purse. "Well, here they are anyway. My former employer, the family I used to live with, a few customers."

"Why are you moving out?" I ask. This seems like a good question, something someone responsible would ask. Perhaps I should ask him where he sees himself five years from now.

"They're moving to Arkansas," Edward says. "They asked me to come. Can you imagine?"

"Well . . ."

Edward wraps his elegant scarf around his neck, slides his coat on. "My sentiments, exactly."

I watch out the window as he drives away. A little navy

blue Toyota. Not a speck of dirt on it. Of course he can move in. Maybe I can borrow his clothes sometime. I head for the bathroom to stare into the mirror and imagine myself as a redhead, dressed smartly.

"YOU MEAN THAT friend of King's?" Travis asks later that afternoon, when he has returned from school. "That Edward?" He pulls a carton of milk from the refrigerator, then takes a drink out of it.

"What have I told you about that?" I say.

"What?"

"About drinking out of the carton?"

"Not to do it." He puts it back on the shelf, closes the refrigerator door.

"So why do you do it?"

He shrugs, sits down at the kitchen table. "I forgot."

"So anyway," I say. "We've got another roommate!"

"What's this guy do?"

What's this guy do? David's influence.

"He's a hairdresser."

"Are you kidding?"

"No, I am not. He owns his own shop."

Travis snorts. "Is he like, *gay* or something?"

"As a matter of fact, he is."

Travis stops smiling, pushes away from the table.

"Where are you going?"

"My room."

"Travis," I call after him. "Come here for a minute."

He turns, reluctantly.

"What's the matter?"

"You're getting really weird, Mom."

"What's that supposed to mean?"

He shakes his head, continues upstairs, slams the door to his room.

I push his chair back under the table. *Am* I getting weird? Well, who should live here? An accountant and his wife and his 1.4 children? I have to take who I can get. I open the door to the freezer, look to see what we can have for dinner. Chicken. Anything weird about that?

LATER THAT AFTERNOON, Travis calls me to his room. I close his door, sit on his bed, and smile at him, sitting at his desk. Finally, "What's up?" I ask.

"I want to live with Dad."

Well, there it is.

"Okay?"

"Travis, what brought this on?"

"I don't want to live here. There's too many people."

"Well, I have to have people living here in order to keep the house. You know that. Don't you want to keep the house?"

"I don't care."

"Well, I do."

He turns away, sorts through some papers, mumbles something.

"What did you say?" I ask.

"You don't have good judgment."

I laugh. "Who told you that? Dad? Did he say that?"

Travis shrugs.

"Listen, Travis. Didn't you like Lydia?"

"Yeah, and she's gone."

"Well, it's not my fault! She got married! But I picked her! That was my judgment that picked her!"

"I *know*! But you also got that crazy girl in the basement! She's *crazy*!"

I sigh, lean back on my elbows. What to say? Perhaps the truth.

"Well, that *was* kind of a mistake. But she doesn't hurt

anyone. She's quiet. Maybe we just need to give her some time."

"I don't want to stay here, Mom. I don't want to *live* with you!"

There, in the center of my chest, a splitting feeling so strong I wonder if something really has split. "Travis—"

"Can I just live with Dad? Please?"

"He can't take you, honey," I say quietly. "He works too late. He can't be there for you after school."

"I don't care."

"But you can't come home alone."

"Yes, I can!"

"Travis, you're eleven years old."

"*Lots* of kids my age come home alone! Way *younger* kids! It's no big deal. I don't even *want* you to be here when I come home!"

"Oh. I see. Well, I didn't know that, Travis."

I really didn't. I need to get away from him right now. I need to cry. I need to punch the too-wide surface of my bed. I need to lean out the window and scream, "Just *wait* a minute!"

"Could you tell me something, Travis? Is it because of the roommates we have here that you want to live with Dad?"

"Not only."

"Okay," I say. "Okay." I go over to kiss the top of his head. "It's okay." And then, on feet that have no feeling, I walk to my bedroom, where I close the door quietly and sit on my bed until the sky darkens, and it is time to make dinner for my son and the crazy girl in the basement who is making us both crazy, too.

Twenty-six

"So kick her out," Rita says. "Big deal. She'll like it, it will confirm everything she believes about life."

"I can't do that."

"Why not?"

"I just can't do things like that. And anyway, she's just a kid!"

"Yeah, like Linda Blair was just a kid in *The Exorcist*. Get rid of her."

"But what would I say?"

"How about, 'Move out, you malcontent? You're ruining my life'?"

I sigh, lean back against my bed pillows, stretch my legs out and look at my toenails. They are newly painted, a deep pink color. The polish was a gift from Edward, a sample he didn't want. Along with about thirty other bottles. I am rich in nail polish. And gels. And sprays. Some of which I gave to my mother, who is suddenly wildly enthusiastic about my choice in roommates. She and Edward get along beautifully. Last time Veronica came for dinner, he helped her on with her coat, reminded her about her appointment for a perm relaxer. "He's darling," she told me on the phone the next day, after she'd returned from the salon. "And his shop is as elegant as his room—the things that man can do in such little space!"

True. Edward has a way of making a place look both warm and contemporary. I wanted him to do my entire house, but he insisted it was fine the way it was. "Just get rid of a few of the philodendrons," he said kindly. Sometimes I stand in Edward's light and airy room for relief after I've been in the basement and have passed by the hellhole that is Lavender's room.

"How's Travis doing?" Rita asks.

"Well, now he wants to stay here, but I think it's only because David didn't really want him there. I mean, he didn't say he *couldn't*, but—"

"Yeah, I know," Rita says. "I know just how he'd do it. All that silky talk about how he'd really love to have him, but his job, his business trips. . . . To say nothing of the fact that he couldn't fuck his girlfriend on the sofa after dinner."

"It's hard for him," I say.

"Oh, please!"

"No, I mean it's hard for Travis. He's gotten pretty friendly with Edward—well, who wouldn't, he's incredibly likeable. But it *is* weird, you know, this rent-a-room thing, all these changing personalities. . . . I'm sure Travis just wants things to be the way they used to be."

"Do you really think so, Sam?"

"Oh, I don't know. I really don't know. One day he's fine; the next day he's awful, and taking everything out on me. Naturally David's always the hero, because he's never here."

"Oh yeah? Well, tell him David wanted to name him Edgar."

"I tried that. He said he likes the name Edgar."

"Oh, he does not."

I look at my watch. "Yikes, I have to go, I have to get ready."

"What are you doing tonight?"

"Actually, just . . . Travis is spending the night with someone, and I was feeling sort of terrible, so I called King. I'm going over there, he's going to make us dinner."

"You're going to his apartment?"

"Yeah."

"First time, right?"

"Yes, and don't get all excited. We're just friends, I told you. And anyway, I think he found a girlfriend."

"He did?"

"Yeah, somebody he met from the personals. He says she didn't get repulsed, so maybe the next time they go out, they'll elope."

"Really?"

"Well, no, but—"

"No, I know not *elope*, but is he . . . serious about her?"

"I think so."

"How does *that* feel?"

I laugh. "*Fine!* We're just *friends*."

Silence.

"We are!" I look at my watch. I probably should get off the phone, we've been talking long enough.

"You know, Sam, once I asked you about something, I can't remember what it was, but I said, 'Well, what are *you* getting out of it?' And you know what you said? You said, 'What do you mean?' "

"What does *that* mean?"

"It *means*, Sam, that at some point you need to start thinking about what *you* want and going after it!"

"I . . . We're just friends, Rita."

"Fine. Call me later. I'm dying to know what his place looks like."

I hang up the phone, shrug off a feeling.

The phone rings again. King.

"Hey!" I say.

"Something's come up," he says. "I'm sorry to call this late. But I have to move our dinner to another night."

"Oh! Okay."

"I'll call you."

I hang up the phone. King's new friend must have called. And why shouldn't he nurture this new relationship? God knows a good one is hard to find.

I go into the bathroom, take the rollers from my hair. Edward did a nice job—he gave me a very pretty color. I realize I'd really been looking forward to seeing what King thought. Well. Another time.

The house is so quiet. Empty—Edward off for the weekend, Lavender out somewhere, too. I go downstairs, look in the refrigerator, put some water on to boil for a hot dog, then turn the burner off.

AN HOUR LATER, I am lying in bed, staring at the wall. Downstairs, I can hear the television I'd tried watching, and then left on for the company of the voices. A commercial is blaring. Well, it's all commercials, even the programs are commercials.

I get up and go to the bathroom to look at my hair again. Awful. What was I thinking? I wet a washcloth, rub it on my hair to see if anything will come off. No.

Back in the bedroom, I stand by the window, arms crossed, looking out. No one is on the street. No one is ever on the street. Everyone stays inside. I wonder what they're all doing, if anyone is acting as lost as I am. What would happen if you could lift the roof—make for a *real* open house—and look inside? What would you see? Surely some of the behavior would be no odder than mine.

Oh, why isn't there a Community Center for People Who Need a Little Something? If people would only tell the truth about the way they felt, it would be busy all the time. There could be folding chairs arranged in groups, people sitting there saying, "I don't know, I just wanted to come here for a while."

I look down at my arm, hold it up to the light to look closely at the flesh. The other day, my skin looked like crepe paper. It still does. It's older, that's all. These things keep happening, these changes that I notice all of a sudden. Yesterday I saw an ad in the newspaper about retirement planning, and I stared at the group of old people, apparently having the time of their lives, sitting around a small table where they were eating dinner. There were three women, one man, all smiling at each other. I tried to put myself in the picture, saw myself in my seventies, desperately flirting. I couldn't imagine it. How will I ever retire? From what? But this is clearly the middle of my life. Next, I get old. My God. It occurs to me that I must have thought I would actually have a choice. "*Next?*" someone with a clipboard would yell. And then, "*Okay! Sam Morrow. So, will it be your fifties next? Or would you like to do your thirties again?*"

Even the imperturbable King seems to have felt the ungentle pressures of middle age, though of his own variety. The other day he showed me a photograph he'd found of some famous astrophysicist, standing outside in what looked to be the Southwest. There were low, violet-colored hills in the distance. On the ground were bushy brown weeds, small rocks, and the imprints the man had made in the dusty soil. The sky overhead was blue and vast, solid-seeming. But a thick line of darkness lay across the foreground, night creeping in.

There was a telescope nearby, aimed upward, graceful and vigilant and ready to reveal the mysteries. But the man ignored it. Instead, he directed his gaze into a baby carriage, where a tiny fist was raised, as though in greeting. The man had one hand on the carriage bar and one hand in his pocket; his feet were planted wide apart, and he was smiling. He looked as though he were at peace, grounded by the more common miracle. "I see this and I just wonder," King said. "I mean, it made me wonder."

"Yes," I said softly. Only *yes*. When what I'd wanted to say was, "What do you mean, though? Do you mean the human connection is stronger? Better?"

I turn from the window, think about what I might do to console myself. It used to comfort me, as a little girl, to look at my mother's jewelry, most of which had been passed down through Veronica's family over many years. I used to try on the heavy gold bracelets, the pearl necklaces, the rings, all at once. I liked pinning the brooches in a line down my chest, the fabric of my shirt sagging from the weight.

I go to get my own jewelry box, sit on the bed with it, take out my wedding ring, try to put it back on. It won't fit. I put it on my little finger, then take it off. Let it be.

I put on my bracelets, all of them, all nine. Here is my double strand of pearls. Tenth anniversary. Ha, ha.

I have quite a few necklaces, too, and I fasten one after another around my neck. Then I go downstairs to get the giant Hershey bar with almonds that I bought yesterday and then put in the freezer so I wouldn't eat it. Well, I'll eat it now. After I eat dinner. I'll have cereal, I want to try some of the heavily sugared stuff I bought Travis, hoping it would make him want to stay with me all the time.

I sit at the table, pour the multicolored cereal into a bowl, add milk. My arm is heavy and sparkling. I like it. *Not lonely, not sad. I'm fine.* And the cereal is good. *I'm fine!* I pour more in the bowl, have another spoonful, close my eyes to taste it better. *But after this, what?* I get up to take the candy bar out of the freezer so it can start defrosting. Then I check to see what else is in the refrigerator *there might be a good movie on TV, there might be a good book around that I bought and never got around to reading, someone may call. Who? Who?* and take a handful of raspberries from a little green carton and pop them in my mouth. Then, recalling that they are Edward's and organic besides, I consider putting them back. *But I can go to the grocery store and get some more to replace them!* I eat a slice of cheese, a rolled-up slice of baloney. Then I sit down again to eat more cereal.

Maybe I should microwave the candy bar; it will never defrost. I drink the milk from the cereal bowl, reach for a napkin to wipe my chin, look up, and see Lavender Blue standing before me.

"Oh," I say. "Hi."

"Yeah, hi," she says. "I just got in." Then, looking at my bejeweled chest and arms, "*You* look nice!"

"Thank you. Would you like some cereal?"

"No thanks." She holds up a book, sighs. "Homework. Although there is absolutely no point in learning about this." She goes downstairs, closes the door after her.

I finish my cereal, put the candy bar back in the freezer, and head upstairs. I take off all the jewelry, put it away. Then I lie on top of my bed, the lights off. Resting before I go to sleep, I suppose. I wish I believed. I wish I could pray.

I get out of bed and onto my knees, bow my head.

Somewhere, a couple lie in bed together holding hands, and they will stay together until one of them dies. They will not hate each other over the breakfast table, they will give thanks for each other's presence. Somewhere, that is true. This is my prayer.

Twenty-seven

KING AND I ARE HAVING DINNER IN HIS TINY APARTMENT. When he called me last night, he confessed he was ill last time we were going to do this, and he was too embarrassed to tell me. Something . . . gastrointestinal.

"Was it—?" I asked.

"Yes," he said, quickly.

King's apartment is furnished with the kind of mismatched but comfortable things you can still find at the Salvation Army. A sofa, a chair, and a reading lamp in the living room. A braided rug. A stereo. A brass iron bed in the bedroom, a white bedspread, a dresser. An old-fashioned bathroom with a claw-footed tub. A kitchen cluttered with cooking tools, bursting with them. And a tiny wooden table, where we now sit.

"I feel like my life is sort of out of control," I say, "like I'm just not doing the right things. But it's odd, because I'm also beginning to feel better than I ever did. Happier, I mean."

"What's wrong with what you're doing?"

"I don't know. Everything. I have such a strange job. And these roommates. My son thinks I'm nuts."

"That's his job. He's pubescent. He'd think you were nuts no matter what you were doing."

"Well, yes. But it's more than that. I feel like I should be . . . more like other people."

"I never saw the percentage in that."

I nod, watch him take a drink of wine. His eyelashes are so black. Long.

"How's it going with . . . Laura?" I ask.

"Linda?"

"Oh. Yes."

"I guess it's all right. I need to . . . Well, there's a lot I want to know."

"And I'm sure you enjoy it, going out. Don't you?"

"I do. But the whole thing is very new. I've never had much to do with women. There was that one time. But that . . ."

"What happened, anyway?"

He looks at me for a long time, considering something. Then he says, "Oh, well. It was a joke. Literally. I'd always been really shy, oversensitive—overweight, too, of course. I'd never tried to date, and then, all of a sudden in my first year of college, there's this really gorgeous girl, after *me*. I couldn't believe it. But she was pretty convincing. And we ended up in her dorm room one Sunday afternoon, and I—"

I say nothing, wait.

"We ended up in bed, and I was so . . ." He laughs. "Well, I got pretty emotional. I thought it meant . . . Well, I thought it was real, and I thought it meant everything. But it was a joke. The girl, Christy was her name, had made a bet with someone. She got a hundred dollars for sleeping with me."

"Oh, King. I'm so sorry."

"Somebody came in just after we finished and took a picture—they'd been standing outside the door the whole time. I guess they passed it all around." He puts down his glass, leans back. "I never told anyone this before. I never thought I would. But it feels kind of good to tell you, Sam. Anyway, after that, I just gave up on ever . . . I let myself get completely taken up by what I was studying. Whatever that longing is, whatever it is that makes people want to be together, I made that need get met by what I learned. Everything is there, in science. Even human emotions, I mean. It's as though they're represented by certain universal laws. Remember when they found the naked stars—did you read about that?"

I laugh. "No."

"You know what a naked star is?"

I think for a minute. And then, I can't help it, I say, "One that just got out of a meteor shower?"

"Very funny. But what they are, are stars with most of their gaseous atmospheres stripped away. And you know why they're revealed like that? Because of close encounters with other stars. I find something very human about that. Don't you?"

I nod. Smile.

"I see that kind of thing all the time. It's thrilling to me. And at the same time, there's a kind of *peace* there, in that kind of contemplation, that you don't get in relationships. At least, I don't think you do."

"Why did you stop?" I ask.

"Stop what?"

"Working at it."

"Oh, I haven't. Not at all."

"But you . . . you know, your job isn't exactly *astrophysics*."

He sits back, looks at me. "Do you ever think about how hard it is to say something and have it be precise?

Especially the things you care most about? You hear the words coming out of you and they are just not quite what you intended. You mean red, you're thinking red, and then out of your mouth comes . . . chartreuse. And you want to take it back, but then the other person is saying, 'Oh, chartreuse, I see,' and it's too late. It's gone. I don't know that in human relationships you ever find the true crossing from here to there. But in physics, it feels like you're getting there."

"But—"

He holds up a finger. "I don't work in it because when I'm away from it in the specific, I'm better able to see it generally. Do you understand?"

I think I do understand. But it's too hard to say how. It's an internal acknowledgment, a yearning kind of stepping forward that will not translate itself into any words that I know. He's right, about the limitations of words. And so I say simply, "I do understand."

He looks at my plate. "Are you finished?"

"Yes, thank you, it was delicious." And it was. Rosemary chicken, garlic mashed potatoes, corn on the cob, sweet peas. A chocolate cake he'd made. From scratch, of course. "Buttermilk's the secret here," he told me. "And you put a little coffee in the batter."

He takes our plates, puts them in the sink, runs water on them. I sit in my chair and watch him, his slow and careful movements, his obvious contentment. There is a low buzz to the overhead light, and the sound is comforting. I want to stand close behind him, lay my head in the shallow valley between his shoulder blades. Instead, I drink more wine.

"Would you like to go into the living room?" he asks, when he has finished rinsing the dishes. A shy formality.

"Yes." He gets his wine, and I follow him into the living room.

"Sit anywhere," he says.

I choose the chair, and he sits at the end of the sofa nearest it. "You know, the thing about the jobs I do . . . A lot of people think I'm lazy."

I say nothing. This had occurred to me.

"But I want . . . time. That's why I walk dogs. I don't want to keep on moving up the ladder, trading in one car for another. I want to be appreciative of all that's here, in a normal life. I want to keep finding out about the things I see around me." He leans forward, looks at me intently. "How do birds know how to fly south?"

"*I* don't know!"

"Yeah, most people don't. *Why* don't you know?"

"Well, I just . . . I guess I just take some things for granted."

"But, Sam, listen to this: They have internal compasses, sensitive to the earth's magnetic field. They calibrate them by sunlight and by the stars. Think of that! Next time you see a bird fly by, think of that! They're everywhere, Sam, these wonders. Do you remember the last time you really wanted to know *everything*?"

The answer comes to me like a movie in my head. I am flat-chested and pigtailed, bending over the edge of a lake and watching the lacelike line of froth advance and recede, trying to determine what makes the water green. The sun is warm on my back. I am entirely unself-conscious—my body is a sack of flesh and bones whose function is to take me where I want to go. On my dresser at home, I have rocks and various kinds of leaves, a jar with a cocoon inside that I inspect a thousand times a day. I am obsessed with discovering things, as though I've been let out of the hatch of a spaceship and told to come back with a full report. For some time, I have nourished a fantasy that a small group of very wise people dressed in close-fitting silver will show up in the middle of my geography class, saying, "We've come for Samantha." And I believe I will rise and follow them, leaving behind forever the lunchbox I am embarrassed about because Veronica always buys the wrong one.

"I do remember when I felt like that," I say. "I was young. A little girl. But strong! I was so *busy*. And then I woke up one morning feeling clumsy and worried to death about which shade of lipstick to wear. And then I woke up the next morning and I was married. And then in labor. And then I had the job of caring for a family, which satisfied me—which is a *sin* now—but which *satisfied* me because *it* seemed to be about everything."

"You were happily walking dogs, so to speak."

"Yes. Yes." I think for a moment, then say, "So . . . you aren't *expecting* anything, are you?"

"I'm just watching the show," he says. "I think it's so good. I don't know why people walk out on it in all the ways they do."

I kick my shoes off, pull my feet up under me. "Einstein didn't wear socks."

"I know."

"That's all I know about physics."

"That's almost enough."

"Oh, God, King. You always make me feel so . . . Like I'm *fine*."

"That's because you are, Sam. How come you don't know that?"

I am embarrassed by a sudden rush of tears. I wipe them quickly away, then laugh at myself. "Oh, jeez, look at *this*."

"Maybe we should go out," he says gently. "Want to see a movie?"

I nod. I felt it, too, a sense that if we took one step further in this direction, we would fall off a cliff together. And I don't know, I still feel made of glass.

Twenty-eight

"CONSTRUCTION?" I SAY. "YOU'RE KIDDING!"

"No, I'm not," Stacy, the woman at the employment agency, tells me. "They're desperate, and I can't find anyone else. It's easy work, the guy says; he says *anyone* can do it. And it pays well."

"But I don't know anything about construction!"

"You don't have to. He'll show you what you need to do. You just put on some old clothes, bring some gloves, and he'll take care of the rest. You want the job?"

"Well . . . Yes."

Stacy tells me the address of the job site, and I go upstairs to change. Bib overalls. A flannel shirt. A ponytail. My hiking boots. All of a sudden, I feel cool.

MARK QUINTON IS killer handsome. The kind of guy who should be posing for calendar pictures for women's fantasies. He's up on a ladder wearing work boots, jeans, a tool belt, and a white T-shirt with *Quinton Construction Company* written beneath a picture of a circular saw. He looks down at me when I come into the room, smiles. "Can I help you?"

"I'm here from the agency. Sam Morrow?"

"You're Sam?"

"Yes."

"I thought you were a man."

"No, I . . . It's Samantha. Did you need a man?"

"No, it doesn't make any difference. Glad to have you." He climbs down from the ladder, comes over to shake my hand. "My partner is sick today, and I'm way behind on this job."

"I have to tell you, I don't know anything about construction."

"Ever used a hammer?"

"Well, *sure.*"

"Then you know something about construction."

I look around the room. Thick sheets of plastic for a roof and walls. Sawhorses, a circular saw resting on one of them. Stacks of lumber, boxes of ceramic tile. Huge quantities of long nails. Large pieces of plywood. Piles of sawdust, a space heater that's doing a great job keeping the place warm. "So. What do you want me to do?"

"First thing is a coffee break," Mark says. "You like cranberry muffins?"

"Yes, I do."

He opens a bag, spreads out a napkin on boards over a sawhorse, sets out two muffins. Then he opens a thermos and pours two cups of coffee into paper cups. "It's got milk in it," he says. "That's what me and my partner like."

"That's fine."

"No sugar."

"Perfect."

"What we're doing is a kitchen/family room," he says. "And what I'm working on today is the roof and the window frames. I need you to take a shitload of nails out of some plywood that I'm going to reuse on the roof. That'll be the first thing. Okay?"

"Fine."

"Then I'll need you to take my truck and run an errand. Go down to the lumberyard and pick up some supplies. You just tell them my name, and they'll load you up."

"Okay." I finish my muffin in two huge bites, gulp down the coffee. "I'm ready."

"You're going to work out fine," Mark says, grinning. He turns on a radio splattered with paint. "You like country and western?"

"Uh-huh."

"You got to hear country and western when you're working construction."

I watch as he shows me how to take the nails out: hammer on the pointed ends until they're almost all the way out; then turn the board over and pry them out by the heads. Put them in the plastic bucket—save them.

I work on this for two hours, then say I'm finished. He comes down, looks at the boards that I've stacked neatly in the corner. "Good." He looks at me, nods. "Come over here, I'll teach you to build a header. That's what goes along the top of the window, to support the weight of the roof."

He lays out two boards of uneven length, tells me to align them at one end, then nail them together. "Here, and here," he says, indicating where the nails should go. "Avoid the knotholes."

I look around nervously. "Are the owners here?"

"Shit, no. Ain't nobody home anymore. People hire me to do these beautiful things to their houses and then they're never in them." He hands me a nail. "This is a tenpenny bright," he says. "Drive it, girl."

I place the nail, tap tentatively at it.

"Use your *shoulder*," Mark says. "Get your *weight* into your swing. And stand off to the side a little."

I do as he tells me and the nail makes its way a good third of the way in. I look up, a little thrilled.

"That's right," he says.

I pound again. It feels so good.

"*Sink* it!" Mark says, and I do.

"I'm not going to tell you what I was thinking while I did that," I say, straightening, my hands on my hips.

"You don't have to," he says, and hands me another nail.

It was nothing about David, what I was thinking. It was about me. I was thinking, "I! Am! *Worth!* Something!"

Mark climbs the ladder, and I finish nailing the boards together. When I'm through, he looks down and says, "See that? You just built a header."

I take a breath. Nod. Nod again.

"Now go and get the keys to my truck, they're in my jacket," Mark says. "Then go to National Lumber—you know where it is?"

I do know. I've driven past it many times, and I tell Mark this.

"All right. Go on over there and tell them you need what I called about this morning. And then we'll have lunch."

"Burger King?" I say.

"Is that what you like?"

"I thought that's what you guys ate all the time."

"I like those tofu roll-ups," Mark says. "But I could do a Whopper."

WE SIT AT a small table by the window at Burger King. Mark is telling me about the time he got kicked out of his Catholic school for falling in love with a nun.

"Are you serious?" I ask.

He nods. "She was real young. And I saw one day that

there were all these little hairs escaping from her wimple. I thought, *whoa!* that's a woman under there! Before that, I thought they . . . I didn't really think they were women. I thought they were a kind of separate species."

"So you saw her hair and fell in love?"

"Well, not right away. What happened was, I was a pretty good artist. And she used to take me outside, up on a hill, and let me draw. And she would just sit with me, read, sometimes she'd read out loud, it was nice. And then one day we started holding hands, hugging a little." He shrugs. "Kissin' . . . Anyway, somebody saw us and I got expelled and she got fired. Never saw her again."

"How old were you?" I ask.

"Twelve."

"Twelve!"

He takes a sip of his Coke. "Yup. I got a son coming up on twelve now. I look at him sometimes, you know? He doesn't tell me anything anymore."

"I know," I say. "They stop."

"Right around ten, they start getting pretty quiet."

"It's true."

"Makes you kind of miss the days when they ran around with their pacifiers, their little tummies hanging over their diapers. 'Member that? Those little belly buttons?"

I smile at him. What a good man.

Mark crumples up his bag. "Ready to go back to work?"

"Yeah." In the truck on the way back, I look at my hands. Two blisters starting. I couldn't be more proud.

Twenty-nine

"I can't do this stupid homework," Travis says. "I hate Mr. Houseman. He's stupid!"

"Let me see," I say, and stop peeling potatoes. At the kitchen table, Travis is holding his forehead in his hands, his usual way of conveying anguish.

He looks up at me, frowns. "*You're* no good in math!"

"Well, just let me see. And for your information, I got an *A* in algebra."

"This is not that," he says.

And it isn't. I don't quite understand what it is. Something close to geometry, though, and I still remember taking my geometry midterm when I was a sophomore in high school. I passed the time by drawing designs for evening gowns on the back of the exam; everything on the front of the page only annoyed me.

"I'm afraid you're failing this class," my teacher had told me later, sadly. He was speaking in a very quiet voice. A whisper, really.

"I know," I had whispered back.

"Why don't you come in after school a few times a week? I'll give you a little extra help."

"Okay," I'd said, thinking, *oh please, no*. But I had gone and Mr. Seidel had patiently drawn angles and worked through proofs, explaining at each step what he was doing and why. For my part, I had watched his hand as he wrote, admiring his neat penmanship, looking carefully at his wedding ring, wondering what his wife was like. When he finally looked up and asked me if I understood, I responded with a blank gaze. He'd given me a *D*-as an act of remarkable kindness.

"Can one of your friends help you?" I ask Travis.

"No."

"Well, call Dad, then. He'll know how to do it."

"He's on a stupid business trip."

"Oh. Right. Well, then, I'm sorry, Travis. I don't know what to tell you. I guess you'll just have to talk to your teacher tomorrow." I go back to the potatoes, out of enemy territory. I'm so glad I'm finished with school. If I were told to go home and spend my evening doing homework—in five subjects, no less!—I'd start screaming.

"Can I call King?" Travis asks.

Of course. Why hadn't this occurred to me?

"Sure. It's 247-8893."

"You know it by heart?"

"Yes," I say. And then, "I mean, it's an easy number."

Travis goes into the family room to make the call. He hates his math class, and I don't blame him a bit. But he's going to have to get through it, or he'll end up like me.

"King knew how to do it," Travis says, coming back into the kitchen. "It's *easy.*"

Well. *His* spirits have improved.

"What's for dinner?" he asks. And when I tell him, he doesn't offer his usual wounded commentary. Yes, his spirits have improved immeasurably.

JUST BEFORE I go to sleep, I rub my hands over my breasts. Pain, on both sides, again. This has been happening a lot, all of a sudden. It can't be cancer. Cancer doesn't hurt. Cancer doesn't show up on both sides. I must be starting to have breast pain when I ovulate. Rita always does. I turn onto my side, burrow into my pillow, think about whether it is time to ovulate. And then I open my eyes wide and lie still as death. I have just figured out my weight gain.

I sit up, slide into my slippers, go downstairs to look at the kitchen calendar with hands that are shaking. No X on any day last month. Or the month before. I press my fingers to my mouth, dry now, sticky. I sit at the table. How could I not have known this? This is exactly what happened with Travis. And I'd been so angry, because everyone else I knew had *lost* weight the first trimester. Not me. My appetite had been amazing. I'd gained and gained.

I push my face into my hands, moan. But then, hearing the front door open, I compose myself. Edward comes into the kitchen, heads for the refrigerator, then sees me.

"*God,*" he says. "I just had the date from hell. Remind me tomorrow to kill myself. What a relief to see *you.*"

Edward is such a pleasant man; I like him so much. He used to be a baby.

I burst into tears.

Edward leaves the refrigerator door open, comes to sit opposite me, takes my hand. "*What?*" he says. "What happened? Oh God, is it Travis?"

"Not exactly," I say.

Thirty

"WELL, I JUST CAN'T BELIEVE THIS," DAVID SAYS. HE IS keeping his voice low; the restaurant is crowded, but I imagine he feels like screaming *"How?"*

It's a fair question. I'm not quite sure myself. But, "In the usual way, David," I hear myself saying. "Sperm meets egg."

"But aren't you too old?"

"Apparently not."

He looks down, stirs the ice in his drink with his fingers. He has such long fingers. I bet this baby has long fingers, too. Travis does. Looking up, David says, "Forgive me. But . . . my sperm, right?"

I sit for a long moment, then say, "No, I don't believe I do forgive you." I stand up, reach for my coat.

He takes my arm. "Please. Don't make this more melodramatic than it already is. We'll take care of it, that's all."

"I'll take care of it," I say. And have the curious sensation, pushing the door open to leave, that two people are doing it.

"OH, GOD," RITA keeps saying, until I finally say, "Will you *stop*? Will you stop saying 'Oh, God'?"

"Well, *Sam*. This is so unbelievable! I mean, it's like

those teenagers who live in trailers and go to the bathroom one day and deliver. And their whole family's standing around with their mouths open saying, *Goooollllleee!*"

"Thank you for your incredible sensitivity."

"Oh, I'm sorry. I know this is . . . Well, I guess this accounts for some of the craziness you've been feeling."

"Who knows? It seems like divorce can do a pretty good job of that all by itself."

"True. Oh, poor Sam. The double whammy. When your hormones get back to normal, you'll probably feel lobotomized. So, when are you going to have it done?"

"What?"

"The abortion."

"I called."

"And?"

"And it's all set. Next week. But, Rita—"

"Don't even say it."

"I have to say it. They asked me these questions over the phone and I just started bawling. 'Any other pregnancies?' Yeah, I've had 'another pregnancy.' It turned into Travis."

"You can't have it."

"Why not?"

Silence.

"I'm raising one on my own. Why not two?"

"Oh, man. Do you need me to go with you? I will. I'll come back out there, we'll go together. When's the appointment?"

"You don't need to come. Thanks, but it's okay."

"Who will go with you?"

"They said it's preferable to bring someone, but you don't have to. They'll assign you someone."

"Great. Rent-a-friend."

"But I'm not *sure*. I want to think about this."

"Don't think about it. Just do it."

"You know, Rita, you're acting like a fucking man. You're not listening, you're just telling me what to do. I'm not sure it's the right thing!"

"Well, fine. But you'd better decide fast."

"I *know* that!"

"Okay. Okay. Look. You know I'll support you in whatever you decide. But I really don't think now is the time. I mean, come on, do you?"

I don't answer. When Travis was a newborn, I would go in to nurse him at night and I would raise his T-shirt to watch him breathe. His stomach moved up and down so rapidly it pained me. I would look at his soft spots, afraid of them, see the pulsations from his beating heart. After a few weeks, he would interrupt himself while he was nursing to look up at me and smile, milk running down his chin. And I would tighten my hold on him, renew my vow that nothing would ever, ever hurt him. This is what I want to tell Rita. But I can't. King is right—the words would only hint at all I mean to say.

"What's David say?" Rita asks.

"What does David say? Yank it out."

"Well, *that's* a little crude."

"When I told him, I felt so . . . We didn't talk much. I wish I *hadn't* told him."

"Why did you?"

"I don't know."

Not true. I know. I told him because I wanted his face to soften and for him to say, "Oh, Sam. That's wonderful. Listen, we'll work it out. I'm not happy away from you and Travis, this was wrong. Let me move back in." And then I would not worry about retirement planning, David could do that. And I would not think that

I would grow old alone and demented in some filthy apartment with a chair by the window.

"I'll let you know," I tell Rita. "I'll tell you when I know."

IN THE DREAM, I am standing by a large tree, the bark with a deeply etched pattern like dried earth. Out of one of the cracks a red tulip is growing. A hand is reaching toward it, ready to pick it. "Oh no, don't," I say. "Don't pick it. It's new life. It's a miracle." I awaken, blink in the darkness, close my eyes again.

Thirty-one

Two days before the appointment, I take a day off from work, tell Travis as he is eating breakfast that I'll be cleaning out his closet today.

"No!" he says, his mouth full of scrambled eggs.

"I have to! You can't shut the door anymore!"

"I'll do it," he says. "You'll throw everything out!"

"First of all," I say, "you won't do it. Secondly, I will not throw everything out."

"Yeah, just the good stuff."

"If you would keep your closet clean, then I wouldn't have to clean it for you. I don't enjoy cleaning it any more than you do. I've told you a hundred times—"

"Oh, don't give me one of your lectures."

"Travis, don't you take that tone of voice with me. I swear to God. Do not speak to me like that again or I'll slap your face. I have never hit you yet, but I promise you I am entirely capable of it."

His eyes widen. "Boy. You're *crabby.*"

"Yes, I am."

"I know!"

"Go to school."

He stands. "I *am!*"

"Fine."

"*Fine!*"

As I watch Travis go out the door, Lavender comes up the basement steps and into the kitchen. "Hi," she says, her voice croaky with sleep.

"Hi."

I watch her grab a spoon, then head for the refrigerator and take out a carton of plain yogurt. She sits at the table and pulls off the lid, smells it. "I really hate this stuff."

"Well, why eat it, then?" I ask tiredly.

" 'Cause everything else is, like, poisonous," she says. "Everything else will give you cancer. The planet is so totally wrecked." She swallows a mouthful of yogurt, shudders.

"Lavender?"

"Yeah?"

"Did you tell Travis that if he eats snow he could die?"

"It's true!"

"And that in a few years we'll all have to wear gas masks?"

She shrugs.

"You know," I say. "I've been thinking. I don't think things are working out too well with you living here."

She looks up, sighs deeply. "You're, like, kicking me out, right?"

"Not 'like.' "

"I knew it."

"I'm sure you did."

"So . . . end of the month, right?"

"Right."

Lavender nods. "This always happens."

"Frankly, I'm not surprised." I want to ask Lavender who her references were. Probably relatives who wanted to make sure she didn't end up with them. But what's the difference?

I go upstairs to Travis's bedroom, sit at his desk, look around his room. He has made his bed, more or less. I reach over to tuck in one edge of the sheet, pull on the quilt to straighten it, find a sock, hold it in my hand. I look out his window, remember when his chin barely came to the ledge, remember him later sitting on my lap while I helped him undress for bed, looking out that same window at the setting sun and saying, with wonder, "The *sky's* coming down." When I came downstairs, smiling, I told David what Travis had said. From behind his newspaper, David said, "Huh. *He's* mixed up."

I open Travis's closet door, stare dejectedly at the mess. It's sort of amazing, the creativity of it. A veritable sculpture of clothes, games, old schoolwork, shoes, hangers, loose felt-tipped markers. Back in the corner is a stack of old children's books, the ones he'd liked best. I pull one off the top of the pile. *Pumpernickel Tickle and Mean Green Cheese*. Ah, yes. I open the book, turn to the picture of an elephant and a boy who are playing cards on the boy's bed. Neither Travis nor I had found anything about that to be unusual. Of course a boy and an elephant are playing cards. What happens next? I close the book, put it back in the closet, shut the door, and go to the phone. "This is Sam Morrow," I say. "I'd like to cancel an appointment."

I AM UP late, watching *E.T.* Couldn't sleep. Suddenly, between my legs, a warm wetness. I go into the bathroom, pull down my pajama bottoms. A fair amount of blood. I go into the kitchen, call the hospital emergency room, speak in a low voice to the nurse on duty. How old am I, he wants to know. Oh. Well, then. I can come in if I want to. Or I can just wait it out. It will undoubtedly all pass without complication. If cramping gets bad, if I develop a fever, if the bleeding doesn't stop . . . Yes, I understand, I say.

I am in my forties. I already have a child. Therefore there is no tragedy here.

I feel more blood coming and go into the bathroom, sit on the toilet and wait. I feel it pass. I stand, and, holding a towel to myself, try to see it in the bloody water. Then I pull up my bottoms and go to the kitchen for a tablespoon. I want to bury it in my yard. I want it always near. But it won't stay on the spoon and I'm afraid to touch it with my hands. I flush the toilet, and, quietly weeping, put on a sanitary pad. It's gone. Everything is gone. I can't hold anything. Back in bed, I cup my hands over my uterus and begin weeping so loudly I awaken Travis. He opens my door, sticks his head in. "Mom?"

I stop crying. "Yes?"

"Are you crying?"

What to say? What not to say? "Yes, I am."

"Oh." He scratches one foot with the other. "Want me to come in there with you?"

I smile, feel tears slide into the corners of my mouth.

"It's okay, honey. Sometimes you just need to cry, right?"

"I guess."

"It's just . . . you know, I was watching a sad movie."

"What one?"

"*E.T.*"

"Oh. The part where he goes away?"

"Yeah. Did you think that was sad, too?"

"Yeah. I guess. Not *that* sad."

"Right. Well, I'm sorry I woke you up. Let's just go back to sleep, okay? And tomorrow let's have something special for breakfast."

"What?"

"Whatever you want."

"Pancakes with blueberries? And bacon?"

"Sure."

"Okay." He starts down the hall, then comes back into my room. "Mom?"

"Yeah."

"I hope you feel better."

"Thank you. I'll be fine."

He hesitates, then comes over to kiss my cheek. Which makes my throat hurt so much I make two fists in order not to cry out.

Thirty-two

"WOULD YOU LIKE TO TRY A SAMPLE OF OUR NEW cheese?" I ask.

The older woman stops her grocery cart, squints at me. "What is it?"

"Well, it's a new kind of Swiss cheese. Much lower in fat than the others."

"Is it any good?"

"Would you like to taste it?"

She frowns. "I don't think so."

I put the foil tray back down on my card table. I'm wearing an apron with a cow on it. I would rather build a header. But this is the only job that was available for me today.

"Would you like to try a sample of our new cheese?" I ask a middle-aged man.

"Does it come with a burger?" he asks.

"No, it's just cheese."

"That was a joke," the man says. "You don't have a very good sense of humor, do you?"

I smile. "Guess not."

LATE THAT NIGHT, before going to sleep, I call King. "I handed out cheese samples today," I say. "What did you do?"

"Painted bedrooms in a new house. Mission white, mission white, and mission white."

"I'm tired of working."

"Good. Let's take a day off tomorrow and go to a movie."

"Two movies."

"Okay."

I hang up the phone and hear the sound of voices, whispering. I get out of bed, come out into the hall. It's Edward and Travis, huddled together downstairs at the front door. "What are you guys doing?" I call down. "It's midnight!"

"Shhhh!" Edward motions frantically for me to come down.

"What is it?" I say, and then, *shhhhh!*ed again, wait until I am at his side to whisper, "What *is* it?"

"I think it's . . . an *intruder*," Edward says, looking meaningfully at Travis. Ah. What he means is, It's a murderer. Edward is clutching his bathrobe at his neck with one hand, wielding his squash racket in the other.

I pull Travis toward me. "You go upstairs. Right now." Tomorrow I'm getting a dog.

"I'm not going upstairs!" Travis says. "He might come up *there*!"

He might. He might be up there *now*. He might have watched me go down the stairs!

"When did you last hear him?" I ask Edward.

"He's outside. I think he's in the bushes."

"Well, what should we do?" I ask. "Should I call the cops?"

"That'll just make him mad," Edward says. And then, "Oh, this is ridiculous! We need a *man* in the house!"

"Mom," Travis says.

"What?" I look at his upturned face and immediately calm down.

"Come with me," I say. "It's all right. Let's go call the police. They'll be right over." I dial 911, then use my best speaking voice, as I am being recorded.

It takes three and a half minutes for the police to arrive. We watch from the window as two overweight men get out of the squad car. The blue flashing lights are a comfort, for once.

"They should be careful!" Edward says. "What are they *doing*, just getting *out* like that!"

"They have guns," Travis whispers. "Probably thirty-eights. Or maybe Magnums."

"What are you talking about!" I say. "What are you talking about guns! That's it, you don't play with Howard Niehauser anymore!"

"Do you mind?" Edward says. "Do you think this is the time and the place? Why don't you wait to see if we live? Then you can kill him."

"Shhh!" I say. I hear it now, too, the rustling of someone in the bushes. And then the police see him, and put their hands, both of them, to their guns at exactly the same time, in the same way. A little police choreography. A little ballet. I start to laugh.

Edward stares at me, bug-eyed.

"I'm sorry," I say. I always laugh when I'm nervous. I hate this about myself.

"Come out of there with your hands up," I hear one of the cops say, and I thrill to the familiarity of the phrase, which, up to now, I've only heard in movies, on TV. A slight figure disentangles itself from the bushes. It is Lavender Blue, who, as she explains hysterically to the policemen, just forgot something, that's all. A statue of Saint Jude she had buried out front when she first moved in. It was just for luck, she tells them as she slides into the car, the muddy patron saint clutched in her hand.

I open the door. "Excuse me!"

One cop slams the car door after Lavender, then heads up the walk toward me. The other cop gets in the front seat of the car and turns around to look at her, a weary sorrow in his face.

"It's all right," I tell the cop who is standing on my front porch. "She used to live here. She just moved out."

"You don't want to file a report?"

"No."

"She always visit this late?" the cop asks.

"She has trouble sleeping."

The cop tongues off a tooth, makes a muted smacking sound. "Okay, then. Take care."

I close the door, turn to see Edward stashing his racket back in the front hall closet. He combs his hair back with his fingers, tosses his head, tightens his robe belt. "Well," he says. "Good night."

"I'm not tired," Travis says, exhausted-looking.

Thirty-three

I'VE GOTTEN TOO DRESSED UP. IT'S ONLY A LUNCH. BUT there was something in his voice.

I see David come in the door, and wave at him. He comes over to the table, smiles. Sits. Smiles again.

The waiter comes over and I order herbal tea. "The same," David says. "You like tea?" I ask. "You never used to."

He shrugs. "It's so cold out. Seems like a good idea."

"It is cold."

"Yes. Sam . . ." A long silence.

I wait. He has circles under his eyes. He's lost a little weight. The waiter brings our tea, and we both order sandwiches. And then David says, "I don't know exactly how to say this. But I've been thinking. Sam, I made a big mistake. I'm coming home."

I sit, frozen.

"Do you think we should tell Travis together?"

"Well, David, I—"

"You don't need to answer right away. We can think about the best way to do it. But I'm just so relieved."

"What about your girlfriend?"

"Oh, that was . . . She was only—"

"Did she leave you?"

He looks into my eyes. "No. It was my decision."

230

He's telling the truth.

I try to imagine telling Travis, think of how happy he will be to learn that his dad is coming back. I can have my old life again.

"I've missed you, Sam. I've come to understand so much about myself lately, about the way we were together, about what we *had* that I just . . ." He stares into his teacup, shakes his head.

"What do you miss, David?"

He looks up, laughs. "Oh, come on, Sam, I think you must know that. Our routines, Travis, I just—"

I swallow, touch his arm. "About me, David. What do you miss about *me*?"

"Well." He smiles, leans forward. "I miss . . . everything. The way you're always there for me. The way you never question me or give me a hard time. Even the meals you make, you—"

"David?" *How about this? The way your shoes are always untied. The way you cry over greeting cards. The way you try to hide your cowlick. The freckle at the side of your right breast.*

"Yeah?"

"It's too late." I pick up my purse. "I'm sorry. But I think it will be better if I just go, now."

"Sam, wait a minute!"

"We'll talk later, David. But not about this. I'm sorry."

I am, a little. I walk down the block, thinking of him sitting there. It's odd; it pains me that his clothes are still so familiar to me. I took the shirt he was wearing to the cleaners many times; I saw the belt and trousers he had on hanging in our closet. I believe I could tell you everything that's in his pockets. But it will happen soon that I won't know anymore.

Thirty-four

SPINACH LASAGNA, KING IS MAKING FOR ME, A GRAND Sunday luncheon, and I'm bringing the garlic bread. I spent the day attempting to make it from scratch, but now that it's out of the oven, I regret the time I spent doing it. It looks awful. I break a piece off the end, taste it. Well, if ever I think about baking bread for a living, I'll remember this. I dump the loaf into the garbage and head for Franco's Market, home of Pepperidge Farm.

When I arrive at King's, he ushers me in with a flourish, bending low at the waist and sweeping a dish towel through the air. He is wearing an apron and, when he stands up straight again, I see that he has drawn on a thin mustache. I smile, reach out to touch it, but he holds his hand up protectively. "Don't mess it up," he says. "It took me a long time to get it so realistic-looking."

His kitchen table has been covered with a red-and-white-checked tablecloth; there are bread sticks in a glass at the center of the table, an antipasto platter, a candle stuck into a Chianti bottle. "Well, this is wonderful," I say, laughing.

"Thank you. Sit down. Would you like some wine?"

In the afternoon? Well, why not? I nod, pull my chair in close to the table, hold up my glass. He fills it halfway with red wine; then, when I don't put the glass down, he fills it to the top. This is my favorite restaurant.

"I'M STUFFED," I say. "My stomach hurts." I am lying on King's sofa, my shoes off, my empty wineglass at my side.

"Yeah, that's how I used to feel after every meal," King says.

"You didn't eat half as much as I did."

"Sure I did."

He's just being gracious. He'd only had two helpings. "You're losing quite a bit, aren't you? I hope you don't mind my asking. *Do* you mind my asking?"

"No, of course not. I've lost forty pounds. Another twenty, I'll have to beat Edward off with a stick."

"Is that what you want to do, lose another twenty?"

"Yeah, I guess."

"That's great," I say. "Although . . ."

"What?"

"Well, I just want you to know that I think you're fine the way you are."

He says nothing, and I look down, feel myself flushing. I shouldn't have said that. He's not losing weight for me.

Finally, to break the silence, I ask, "Do you like having no curtains?"

"I never thought of it. Do I need them?"

"I don't know. No. I like how everything's so . . . simple here."

"I've never been much of a decorator. My parents weren't either. What we did was read. You know, at dinner and everything."

"Do your parents live near here?"

"No, they died, both within the last couple years. My dad was at a bookstore, looking at an atlas. He'd wanted a new one. And my mom had a heart attack exactly a year later."

"I'm sorry; I'd thought they were still around."

"Yeah, I'm sorry, too. Because they would have been really happy. They always wanted me to—"

The doorbell rings and I sit up, slide into my shoes. I don't know why. I guess I'm afraid it's Travis, checking up on me. "Why are your shoes off?" he'd say.

But of course it's not Travis. When King opens the door, I see a willowy blond woman, very attractive, smiling.

"Linda!" King says.

Oh.

"I thought I'd surprise you," she says, and I hear the confident lilt of flirtation in a relationship that is going well. "What's on your lip?" she says, reaching up to wipe it away. Then, seeing me, "Oh. You're busy."

I stand. "It's okay. Come on in. I'm Sam. I'm just a friend." I regret having eaten so much, not having worn mascara.

King steps aside. "Yes, come in."

Linda enters, but stands by the door. "I can't stay, really. I just wanted to drop a book off." She hands a small volume to King, and he smiles, thanks her.

I want a coat like Linda's. It's camel-colored, with a collar that you can stand up high. Her boots are a rich brown, high-heeled. Well, that's just silly. High-heeled boots. Ridiculous. Make up your mind, sexy or safe. Large gold hoop earrings, too, I see, watching Linda push her hair back. Catch something in there and say good-bye to your lobe. I could have blond hair, too, if I wanted. A word to Edward, and voilà. Last week he "tipped" me. Very elegant. Linda's lipstick color is nice, but her blush is too obvious. Plus the woman is stupid, I can tell just by looking at her. King can do much better than this. I'll tell him. I owe it to him. As a friend.

There is a sudden silence, and I realize something has been said to me. "Pardon?" I say, smiling an awful, fake smile. My chest hurts.

"I just said it was nice to meet you," Linda says. "I hope I'll see you again."

"Oh! Yes! I hope so, too!"

After King closes the door, I sit back down. "Well! She's very nice."

"Yeah."

"She's the one you met from the personals, right?"

"Right."

"So, what does she do?"

"She's a teacher."

Nursery school. Of course, she's exactly the type. I see Linda in her high-heeled boots, hop-hop-hopping around in a circle with her class, all of them being rabbits. Noses twitching. Bent hands for ears.

"She teaches at Boston University."

Okay, freshman English. "What does she teach?"

"Quantum mechanics."

"Oh, uh-huh. Well, that's . . . So, what book did she bring you?"

King hands me a volume of Shakespeare's sonnets.

"You like these?" I ask.

"Sure. Don't you?"

"I never understand them." I clear my throat. Smile.

I need to go home. In the hamper are about forty loads of wash. And I need to pay the bills. There are many bills. Stacks and stacks of them.

"Shakespeare's not so hard," King says. "You can understand this." He opens to a page. "Here: 'Rough winds do shake the darling buds of May.' Nothing hard about that, right?" He sits beside me on the sofa, points to the line, says it again. "See? And they are, aren't they? Darling? The buds?"

I stare into my lap. His breath is like licorice. Why is his breath like licorice? Mine is like a garlic factory, I'm sure. Not that there is such a thing. A garlic factory. I think about it anyway, imagine blond-haired girls wearing braids and white uniforms standing on an assembly line, shaping cloves into bulbs.

Then I look up at him. His breath is like licorice and his apartment is overly warm because he knows that's how I like it and his hand is under my chin and he is going to kiss me.

"King."

He sits back. "I'm sorry."

"No, it's . . . I mean, aren't you . . . sort of . . . involved?"

"With Linda?"

"Yes!"

"I think *she's* sort of involved."

"I'd say so." I stand, head for the kitchen. "Come on, I'll help you clean up."

He follows me. "You don't have to."

"No," I say. "I want to. Really. I like washing dishes."

I wash and he wipes. For a long while, we don't talk, just stand, hips nearly touching, quietly working. And then I draw in a breath, take my hands out of the dishwater and put them on King's shoulders. And do not understand how he knows how to kiss like that.

I reach around him and untuck his shirt, wonder if I really mean this. I pull away from him, look into his face. "Are you— Is this okay?"

He nods.

"Should we—?"

He nods again, takes my hand and leads me to the bedroom. There, he carefully folds down the blankets, fluffs the pillows. And then he starts to unbutton his shirt, but stops. "I don't know . . . I mean, do I—?"

"Yes."

He doesn't move.

"I'll tell you what," I say. "Let's just talk. But lying down."

His relief brightens the room. I lie beside him, stretched out on my side. He is on his back, his eyes closed. Now that we've decided to slow down, I'm dying to speed up. I put my head on his shoulder, my hand on his chest. He is more solid than I had imagined. I unbutton two buttons, wait, then rise up to look into his face. "Okay?"

"Yes," he says. And then we don't talk anymore. And when I get home, I look at myself in the mirror to see if what I feel shows. What I see is the faint transfer of King's mustache, and I wash it off with regret.

AT EIGHT O'CLOCK, Travis and I are watching TV when Edward comes home. He nods hello, hangs up his coat, then comes to sit on the sofa beside us. At the commercial, Travis goes into the kitchen, and Edward leans toward me. "What happened to *you*?" he whispers. And then, when I don't answer, he leans back, arms crossed, smiling. "That's what I thought."

"What?" I say. "You don't know anything."

"Oh, *please*."

I stare at him. "Your teeth are going to get all dried out if you don't stop smiling. And then your lips will stick to them, and you'll look like a chimpanzee. Stop smiling!"

"*You're* not."

* * *

AT MIDNIGHT, STILL awake, I call Rita.

"We did it!" I say.

Rita gasps. "Tell me everything. *Everything*. Wait! First I want to go get a glass of wine."

"Okay, I will, too."

I go quietly down to the kitchen, pour myself a glass of wine, and head back to my bedroom, closing both Travis's and my door.

I get under the covers, pick up the phone. "Are you there?"

"Yes! Tell me everything!"

"Okay." I lie back against the pillows, take a sip of wine, wonder where to start. I see King's face over me again, a tenderness there that made me separate into two selves, one who lay in a warm bed held by warm arms and another who looked down and nodded. He had run his hands over my breasts so gently, so tentatively. And then his mouth was on me and moving down, so slowly. And when finally he put himself inside me, he froze for a moment, his breath held, his eyes fixed on mine, and then there was no separation of anything. For the first time in my life, I had the sensation of simultaneous giving and taking so huge there was no room for anything else, anywhere. It was less sexual than sacred, close to what I think a good death might be. He had wept a little afterward, saying that he was afraid to believe it could ever happen like this, that he was so grateful that I was the one, that he was sorry he was weeping, he didn't know why he was weeping, he felt terrific, he felt like running outside and lifting up cars. And I held his giant shaggy head on my chest and stroked his hair and said that was fine, I would be happy to help him, so long as the cars were small. And then we had done everything again. And then he had said he was sorry he still weighed so much, he would lose more, he hadn't hurt me, had he? And I said no, he had not.

"Rita?" I say.

"Yeah?"

"I think I don't want to tell you. I mean, it was wonderful. I just don't want to tell you the details. I feel like . . . it's ours."

Silence. And then Rita says, "Sam?"

"Yeah?"

"Do you have your glass of wine?"

"Yeah."

"Well, hold it up, girl, and let's have a toast."

Thirty-five

"WHY ARE YOU MAKING THINGS SO FANCY?" TRAVIS asks. "Who's coming?"

"Mom and Lydia."

"That's all?"

"Yes."

"Why don't you just do things regular, then?"

"Because *they're* fancy."

A horn honks outside. Travis doesn't move.

"There's Dad," I say.

"I know."

"Well . . . Are you ready?"

"Yeah. Are you having that cake you made for dinner?"

"Yes."

"Is it King's recipe?"

"Yes. I'll save you some. Okay?"

The horn honks again. "Go, honey. Don't keep him waiting."

He lifts his duffel bag, shoulders it. "It's more fun here."

How should I feel about this? I'm glad. I'm sad. But I'm glad. And I know that sometimes the cake will be sitting on David's counter, too.

I go to the door with Travis, kiss him good-bye, wave to David, hurry back to the kitchen.

I have just put in the bread to warm when the doorbell rings, and then I hear my mother yoo-hooing her way down the hall. I kiss her, then Lydia, then lead them to the lavishly decorated dining-room table, where they exclaim softly over everything. Travis is right. It is fun here.

WE ARE SITTING back in our chairs, satisfied, empty dessert plates before us. Lydia is talking about her oldest grandchild, who lives in Seattle and who visited her yesterday. "He's almost forty, and do you know he still goes to see if I keep his little black plastic horse in my night stand? He left it at my house when he was just a little guy, maybe two or so, and I put it in my drawer to keep for him until the next time I saw him. But he liked that it was by my bed, and he told me to keep it there for him. Every time I've seen him since, he's asked to see it. 'Checking on the livestock,' he calls it."

This makes sense to me. I once spent hours in Veronica's basement, looking through scrapbooks. I found drawings that Louise and I had done over the years, and I actually counted, making sure Louise didn't have more in there than I did. We were exactly even. I suppose you always want someone to prize things about you.

I have a footlocker for Travis's drawings, his schoolwork, art projects. Although he is hardly sentimental about it. He looked through it one day, then asked, "What do you keep all this junk for?"

"You might want it someday," I told him.

"What for? It's embarrassing!"

"It won't be when you're forty."

"Yeah, right. Like I'll be able to even *see* when I'm *forty*!"

I stared at him, open-mouthed, and he left the room.

"How's married life, Lydia?" Veronica asks.

"Oh, we're very happy. Thomas is a wonderful man. I feel lucky to have found him, and I'm so glad to have taken the chance all over again. Not a single regret."

My mother smiles, looks down at her plate.

"You were very happy in your marriage, too, weren't you?" Lydia asks my mother.

"We were. Sad to say, I think that's a rare thing. I think most young people today are so focused on tomorrow they forget all about today. And I think they're as afraid of happiness as they are of pain! Scared to say they care. Scared to take a chance. Scared to say they're just as sentimental and full of human need as people always have been and always will be."

"It's true," Lydia says, stirring her tea.

They are leaning toward each other, nodding, in complete agreement. I suppose I'm one of the "young people" they're referring to. One of those scaredy-cats. But I did admit to my own needs, to my own sentimentality. And look where it got me.

"You know," Veronica says, "I was over visiting a girlfriend the other day and her father was staying with her, this old geezer who used to be a farmer. Really nice old man. Blind now, but not a bit sorry for himself. He sat down with us and was telling us about life on the farm. Said he still dreamed about it, that in his dreams he could still see. Said he could ask for what he wanted to dream about, too, and oftentimes, it would happen."

"Really!" Lydia says. "I'd love to be able to do that!"

"Well, me, too. You can imagine! I'd be with my husband every night! Anyway, this guy said that he'd asked his dreams to let him see his wife again, and sure enough, it happened. He saw a time after they were first married.

They were out on the front porch, thinking of all they were going to do, just sitting on the wooden steps, holding hands, the sun going down, talking about how they'd have babies till the plumbing quit. He said the lilacs were out, and the smell was so sweet it could bring a dead man back to life. His wife let her hair out of its bun, shook it all loose. And she looked over and smiled at him, and he said, 'Lord, she was so pretty and she was my wife.' Well, my friend and I just couldn't say a word, all choked up. Just seeing him, all those years ago, thinking life was longer than it is. But you know, he said that at least he knew right then that it was a good moment. Said mostly you don't know, in this life, you don't know when it's happening. You look back later and say, Oh! Well now, *that* was a good *time*! But he said he knew it then. Said he knew it lots of times. He said, 'Yes, sir. I've been blessed.' "

"Well, that's just how I feel," Lydia says.

My mother looks at me and I nod. I know that despite everything she lost, she feels the same way. And wants me to, as well.

I see us, suddenly, as though from above, three women sitting around a dining-room table, our mother's hands folded in our laps, our lipstick faded from our mouths. All around us clocks ticking, stars shining. They used to be my age, and I will soon be theirs. They have never forgotten the reason to love.

I don't know what I'm waiting for.

I look at my watch, start to speak. "Go," my mother says.

Thirty-six

NO ONE ANSWERS WHEN I KNOCK AT HIS DOOR. I TRY IT, find it open, and put my head in. "King?" And then, louder, *"King?"*

"Sam?" I hear back, faintly. "Wait just a second. I'm in the bathtub."

I take off my coat and my boots, undress as I walk down the hall, enter the bathroom naked. He is standing on the bath mat, a towel wrapped around him. "Oh. Hello," he says. "Wow. Nice outfit."

"Get back in the bathtub," I say. And when he does, I climb in, too. I lean against his chest, watch water cascade over the side. "Oops," I say lazily. It's pretty, the sight of the brief little waterfall.

"Is the water too hot?" King asks.

"No, this is just how I like it."

He picks up the soap, and I watch his big hands in front of me, lathering up, then rubbing across my breasts, my stomach. "King?"

"Yes?"

"Do you think you could love me?"

His hands stop moving. "You mean . . . now?"

"No, I meant . . . generally."

He sighs, and for a moment I feel as though my insides are shrinking, folding in on themselves. I shouldn't have asked. It's too soon. But then I hear him say, "Oh, Sam. What else would I do with you but love you forever?"

I sit so still I can hear him breathing, and he is breathing very quietly. I think of a conversation I had with Edward recently. I was sitting at the kitchen table and he was standing over me, trying out some fancy hairdo. He was saying how similar King and I were, that it was no wonder we liked each other so much. "I mean, you were both running around with your helmets on backward," he said, "living lives that were totally oblivious. Thank God you met each other so you could wake *up*!"

"I wasn't oblivious," I said, and Edward said, "Oh, come on, can't you see the difference in yourself?"

"Well," I said. "I know how to change a furnace filter now, if that's what you mean. I can unstick a garbage disposal."

"Oh, I think it's a bit more than that," he said.

So it is.

I lean in closer to King, close my eyes, and suddenly I am a little girl again, sitting on the grass outside my house one hot summer day, resting after a solitary game of hopscotch. There are Johnny-jump-ups growing out of the cracks in the sidewalk; the clouds are circus animals; there is lemonade in the refrigerator; my shorts are a fine, faded red. My father is due home at any moment, and I like to watch him get out of the car and take long strides toward me, his face full of loving intention. I run to him, and he lifts me up. And then, together, we go inside, toward whatever else might follow. We are full of faith, blessed by it. I remember, now.